Carl entered,

took three paces forward, snapped to attention, and saluted. Then the feeling of shock hit the pit of his stomach as he saw who else was in the room.

Captain-Chevalier Higgins was behind his desk.

On the observers' platform were seven Guests: a pair of beetles, a creature with three legs and a tall eye-stalk, three squat, pug-faced, massively muscled types that smelled vaguely of methane, and the girl guest, Alyssaunde.

To Captain-Chevalier Higgins' right were two aides-de-camp and His Most Righteous and Honorable Majesty, Hiram the Sixth, by the grace of God King of the Celts and Picts and Jutes, Emperor of Rome-in-Exile, and Hereditary Foe of the Supremacy of Allah.

"At ease, Corporal," Higgins said. "You know why you're here?"

"No, sir," Carl said, fighting a sudden impulse to scream. . . .

But screaming would not have helped —not when action was necessary!

TOMORROW KNIGHT

Michael Kurland

DAW BOOKS, INC.
DONALD A. WOLLHEIM, PUBLISHER

1301 Avenue of the Americas
New York, N. Y.   10019

COPYRIGHT ©, 1976, BY MICHAEL KURLAND

All Rights Reserved.

Cover art by Douglas Beekman.

FIRST PRINTING, FEBRUARY 1976

1 2 3 4 5 6 7 8 9

DAW BOOKS

PRINTED IN U.S.A.

TOMORROW KNIGHT

❊ 1 ❊

The Second Corps of His Most Imperial Majesty's Holy Crusade was drawn up for battle. The heavy cavalry, three hundred Grand Knights in full armor, took their place at the center of the line. The light cavalry, chain mail glittering in the early morning sun, stretched out on both sides of the center to the two edges of the field of battle. Behind the horsemen, the infantry, a wall of soldiers six men deep, stood with pikes at port as their sergeants strode back and forth between the ranks pulling the eternal last-minute inspections.

From his position at the head of his platoon on a small hill at one side of the field, Lance Corporal Carl Frederic Allan had a fine view of this spectacle. He watched as Duke Edgar, the corps commander, and his staff rode up the line in a final review before taking their places at the head of the Grand Knights.

Flipping away his cigarette, Corporal Allan turned away from watching the battle formation. Holding the reins tightly in his right hand, he adjusted the chinstrap on his helmet with his left. As the moment for the attack grew nearer, the horses sensed the tension in the air and grew increasingly nervous. Corporal Allan checked his wristwatch and then leaned over in his saddle and tapped the man to his left. "Unfurl the banner," he said.

"Right, Corporal," the trooper said, and released the

leather thong which held the unit flag tightly furled against the staff. "How long now?"

"About seven minutes. Pass the word down the line." Corporal Allan glanced up at the flag fluttering uneasily in the light breeze and nodded satisfaction. The Horde of Allah would know who was attacking them. The words *Eleventh Light Mounted Infantry Attack Company*, superimposed over the crusader sword-and-shield emblem of His Most Imperial Majesty Hiram VI, with the motto *Never Dishonored* underneath. A truly satisfactory battle flag.

Below them on the field the signalman sounded Up Tails All on the trumpet, and the Grand Knights clicked their helmet visors down. Carl Frederic gave his men a final appraisal. "Wilkens! Put out that cigarette!"

"Sorry, Corporal." The offending butt was cast aside. In the distance, on the far side of the battlefield, the thin, reedy whine of a Saracen war-horn set the Horde into motion toward the crusaders. A few seconds later the Emperor's Call to Battle sounded a defiant answer. The Second Corps moved out to meet the enemy.

As a unit, paced at the speed of the marching foot soldiers, the moving mass lumbered across the field. At the same pace, from some two miles away, the Horde of Allah approached.

It was, as Carl Frederic observed critically from his vantage point on the hill, a glorious morning for a battle. The flitterboats were out in force over the battle area. Mostly the bright, randomly mottled boats of the Guests, but a few of the severe red-and-gray craft of the Inspectors were darting over the field.

One of the flitterboats, colored mostly a violent pink, swooped low over Carl's platoon and startled the already nervous horses. *Damn dung-headed fool*, Carl thought as he steadied his jittery mount, *watch but not interfere indeed! If that's not interference I'm a* . . .

"Move in line—column forwaaard!" Captain-Chevalier Higgins, the commander of the Eleventh, waved his hand once around his head and pointed forward. The flag bearer left Lance-Corporal Allan's side in front of the Third Platoon and rode to the head of the company, taking his place on the commmander's right, and the Eleventh Light Mounted Infantry Attack Company—Never Dishonored—dogtrotted into battle.

With the armies approaching each other at a walking pace, it would be ten minutes yet before they engaged; this gave Commander Higgins about eight minutes to get his men into position for the special battle plan. The Eleventh was usually a primary reserve force, used to meet and stop any enemy unit that broke through the main line; but this morning Captain-Chevalier Higgins and the Eleventh were under special orders.

The unit wheeled into position on schedule, and the plan went into operation. The archers, back row of the infantry, knelt and sent a barrage of arrows over their lines and into the enemy ranks. The entire mass of cavalry, light and heavy, charged the Saracen lines, raising a cloud of dust that almost obscured the battle area. A few of the Guests' flitterboats ducked in close to get a better view of the first clash, and Carl Frederic could see the arrows bouncing off the boats' force screens.

Now the special battle plan went into operation. The first line of Grand Knights released thongs on their saddles that dropped blankets on the ends of ropes, to be pulled behind their charging horses. Under the cover of the thick dust cloud that instantly covered the whole field, the rest of the Grand Knights, the main body of heavy cavalry, swung sharply to the right and raced down the aisle between the first and second row of light cavalry. The Eleventh and Fourteenth Light Mounted Infantry Attack Companies closed in to fill up the gap in the center of the line.

A minute later the two armies met. The Horde's heavy armor broke through the thin line of Grand Knights and into the midst of the Eleventh and Fourteenth. A long, black helm with a Saracen tuft on top appeared in front of Carl Frederic, and he took a vicious swing at it with his sword. The sword bounced off the heavy plate and the Saracen turned, spinning a massive, ugly chain-mace about his head, his eyes glittering through the slits in his helm. Carl thrust his sword up with both hands, meeting the mace's chain near the handle. The heavy, spiked ball at the end of the chain bucked back, knocking Carl's sword from his grasp, and smashed into the top of the black helm. The Saracen slumped in his saddle.

Carl Frederic swung from his saddle and dropped to the ground, keeping his eye on his sword where it had been flung by the bucking mace. In two steps he had it in his hand again. There was no time to remount, nor any real point to it. Horses were good for quick movement, but for stationary fighting a man needed his own two feet on the ground. To Carl's right Commander Higgins was trying to hold off two heavily armed Saracen Grand Knights, who had him pinned between their great war-horses. Carl lunged at the nearest one, trying to unseat him with the sword. The point caught in a crack in the Saracen's armor, and, as the man swiveled, Carl's sword broke neatly in half. Carl cursed and threw the useless handle aside. He grabbed the Saracen around the waist and climbed up the armor like a man scaling a mountain. The Saracen tried to push or beat him off, but he couldn't get his sword into play because Carl was too close; that immobilized the sword hand, since the Saracen was not willing to drop his sword. Before the man inside the mountain of armor could figure out any effective counter to Carl's unorthodox attack, Carl had the leverage and had pulled him out of the saddle. They hit the ground together, side by side.

Carl rolled and leaped to his feet. The black knight tried to get up, but was unable to move at anything beyond a turtle's pace because of the weight of his armor. Left alone, he could have eventually stood, but every time he reached his knees, Carl Frederic pushed firmly with the heel of his foot against the black knight's breastplate, and he clattered back to the earth. Carl quickly tired of this game, but there was no weapon he wore which would pierce the black night's armor, and he did not care to leave the Saracen behind him. Horses were charging back and forth around him, men were yelling and racing by; the dust concealed all beyond a few feet from him, and Carl had no idea of how the battle was coming or who, if anyone, was winning.

Car backed off and circled around the black knight, who rolled over and twisted around to keep him in view. It was a stalemate, and could last until the end of the battle unless one of them did something clever or assistance emerged from the dust cloud. Carl tried to think of something clever as he kept circling. Then he tripped over something, tried to fall as he had been taught in training, and wrenched his shoulder. *Fine*, he thought, *great! I don't need an enemy, I can maim myself quite without assistance*. He backed up to see what he had tripped on. It was a massive Saracen war-ax, blade bit deeply into the iron-hard ground, haft sticking up at a slight angle. Carl took it in both hands and tried to yank it free. It refused to budge and sharp pains shot through his shoulder. The Saracen was back up to his knees.

By now the main body of the battle had moved away from Carl and the Saracen knight, and the dust was beginning to settle around them. The noise in the near distance—yells, screams, moans, thumps, thuds, horses' hooves, and the constant clanging of metal on metal like an army of busboys dropping their trays—made speech or thought equally difficult. "Yield!" Carl Frederic screamed at the Saracen, tugging at the war-ax, but the Saracen, oblivious, continued the struggle to stand erect. He had one foot up now and was ready to push up and stand.

"Yield!" Carl Frederic demanded again, leaving the war-ax and leaping feet-first toward the black knight. His feet hit the black knight in the chest, bowling him back on the ground with an impressive clank. Carl landed heavily on his side a few feet away, and lay there for a minute breathing heavily and holding his shoulder. "Yield!" he panted.

"Your father was a cook!" the Saracen yelled, once again starting the process of standing erect in armor.

Carl pulled himself to his feet and went back to the war-ax. He stood on the handle, and it sank a couple of inches. Then he lifted it to its former position and stood on it again. After a few more loosening stands, he worked it back and forth like a pump-handle, and it came free. "Yield!" he yelled again, advancing toward the kneeling Saracen and waving the ax around his head.

The black knight thought about this for a second and then nodded. "You're on," he said, his voice muffled by the helm. He lifted the faceplate and fastened it back. "A war-ax I can surrender to," he said calmly. "Why didn't you think of that sooner? I couldn't quit as long as you were just jumping up and down on me. Code of battle and all that."

"I had to find the stinking ax, didn't I?" Carl said reasonably. "Hold out your hand." The Saracen complied, and Carl took a small stamp and pad from his pouch and stamped:

PRISONER
fairly taken in open battle
by C. F. Allan, Corporal
Eleventh L.M.I.A.C.
Never Dishonored

in red indelible ink across the back of the knight's hand. "Well, you're out of it now," he said.

"It is no disgrace for a Grand Knight to be captured by a mounted infantryman," the Saracen said. "But it certainly is a calamity. I won't see any bonus money for the next year, that's for sure."

"Sorry, pal," Carl Frederic said.

"Sure you are!" the Saracen snarled. He pulled his long, red capture sash from inside his armor and, wrapping it around his neck, stood up and clanked his way off the field.

"At least you're alive," Carl yelled at the retreating back. "Would you have preferred me to bash you with the ax?" The Saracen ignored him, and Carl turned and, hefting the ax over his shoulder, headed toward the closest clump of fighting bodies.

As Carl approached the clump he could make out what was happening: a group of about nine or ten black knights had surrounded four or five Grand Knights and were hacking away at them, trying to break through their circle. Another few steps closer and Carl could see that the Grand Knights were the Life Guards of Hiram VI, and the white-plumed knight in the center was His Majesty himself, standing firm and laying about him with a great two-handed broadsword. Above the double circle three curious flitterboats had descended and were hovering barely out of reach of the arc of the great sword-blades.

Swinging his war-ax around his head and yelling at the top of his lungs, Corporal Carl Frederic Allan charged into the midst of the Saracens. The bright steel ax-head whistled as he brought it around and contacted the shoulder piece of the nearest black knight with a shuddering crunch. The Saracen slumped forward and dropped to the ground as if his strings had been cut, and the ax flew out of Carl's grasp, striking another black knight on the back of the helm. The ax-blow had done something to Carl's right arm, and it dangled uselessly from the shoulder and throbbed.

The second black knight had also dropped, and two of the remainder turned to face this new threat. Carl pulled his eight-inch dirk from its scabbard and, holding it in front of him with his left hand, retreated slowly from their broadswords. If one of them would suggest surrendering, he would seriously consider it.

With a mighty bellow, Hiram VI brushed aside the Saracen belaboring him and strode to the two black knights advancing on Carl. Grasping the hilt firmly in both hands, His Majesty smashed both Saracens across the side of the helm with the flat of his broadsword, knocking them silly. "Hiram the Mighty," His Majesty said, chuckling heartily, as the two knights crumpled to the ground, knocked cold.

"Thank you, Sire," Carl said gratefully, trying to do a proper bow and failing miserably.

"Nonsense, thank *you*, lad," Hiram boomed before striding away.

Carl Frederic suddenly found that he was very dizzy. Then everything unfocused and went dark, and he felt himself falling.

❃ 2 ❃

The next time Carl noticed anything, the sun was setting and he had a dreadful headache. "Must have fallen asleep," he muttered inanely as he staggered to his feet. "Better get back to the bivouac." He looked around trying to figure out where he was and which way to go. The battle appeared to be over, although it was impossible to tell which side had won. The dead and wounded seemed to have been cleared up, too; at least there were none in sight. Carl, quite obviously, had been overlooked by the clean-up crew. He would speak to someone about that, after a good night's sleep and a couple of aspirin.

Carl started trudging along in the direction he fondly hoped was homeward, looking over the ground he traversed to see if any of the litter of battle he passed was unbroken enough to bring a price as a souvenir. The Guests were fond of souvenirs. Carl found a couple of crossbow bolts and a light, curved reserve sword of a Saracen pattern before it was too dark to make out small objects on the ground.

Carl was too sore to walk far or fast, although no bones seemed to be broken, and a short while after dark he sat down to rest. Although the camp couldn't be more than three or four miles away, he was beginning to doubt whether he'd make it before breakfast.

A thin slice of moon was rising from the Altoona Mound, forbidden ground except to Guests, the stars were beginning to appear, and there was a cold breeze blowing. Carl thought briefly about spending the night where he was, then decided he'd better make it back to bivouac or he'd certainly catch pneumonia and spend the next month flat on his back in the infirmary. The quality of empathy in the infirmary was not great, and rumor had it that the doctors worked on troopers until they had enough experience to go off and work on real people like officers or civilians. Carl got up and started walking again.

"Want a lift, soldier?" The question came from behind him, in a girl's soft voice, and frightened him more than the Saracen's chain-mace had.

Carl wheeled, and stared into the great front viewport of a flitterboat. It was hovering three feet off the ground, and its open door spilled a cone of yellow light onto the mangled turf.

"Well, do you want a ride or not?" It wasn't a girl at all, it was a Guest. A very human Guest, but still a Guest, and not to be considered a girl by any trooper who happened to notice her. If he could have considered her a girl, Carl would have considered her a very pretty girl indeed: long brown hair fell in waves to below her shoulders, and her slender body curved in very girlish ways beneath her simple gold tunic. But she was a Guest. Could he accept a ride from a beautiful female Guest? What did the Rules say? He couldn't remember.

"Come on," she said. "Make up your mind. If you want a lift, get in; if you'd rather walk . . ." Carl cut off the rest of her sentence by jumping in the flitterboat.

"Yes, miz. Thank you. I'll ride."

"I thought you' never make up your mind." She patted the bucket seat next to her. "Stop looking so nervous and sit down, I won't bite."

"I'm not nervous," Carl said stoutly. "It's just that— Well, I've never been in one of these before."

He put his booty down on the floor in front of him and gingerly lowered himself into the seat.

"What, never been in a flitter? What a shame, they're so much fun. Fasten your belt!" She reached across him and pulled a wide piece of webbing from one side of his seat and attached it on the other. In the process her arm touched his, and the beautiful perfume of her body clogged his nostrils.

She's a Guest! The alarm reaction cut in, and doors thudded closed over certain whole areas of consideration in his thoughts. He stared rigidly ahead.

The Guest laughed a golden laugh, oblivious of her effect on him. "Flitters are much less restricting than horses," she said. "Watch!" She pushed a button on the panel by her left hand and the door slid closed. Then, resting her arms on the armrests of her seat, she grasped the control handles built into the front of the rests. She pulled back slowly on both of them.

Carl was entirely unprepared for what happened. He should have anticipated it, of course, he had watched flitterboats all his life; but doing and watching are two different things. The flitter started going faster and faster and the ground dropped farther and farther below. Carl felt an oppressive tightness in his chest, and then discovered that he'd been holding his breath. The girl played delicately upon the knobs, buttons, switches, and sticks built into the armrests of the chair, and the flitter twisted, jogged, looped, spun, lifted, and dropped in an intricate, unpredictable pattern. Carl fought to keep down the little food he had eaten in the past twenty-four hours. The flitter stopped dropping when it was five feet above the ground, and a giant hand tried to shove Carl through the floorboards.

"They don't eat grass, either," the Guest remarked.

Carl gulped. "Pardon me?" He watched the Guest's slender hands closely to see that they kept away from the controls.

"Flitters—they don't eat grass. Horses eat grass."

"Oh, yes, miz," Carl said, not too sure of what they were talking about. "What do they eat?"

The Guest giggled, and it was a joyous, sparkling sound. "Very good," she said. "I'm glad you can keep your sense of humor while you're losing your—equability. Did you know you'd turned green on that last roll?"

"Miz?"

"Positively green," she said, amused.

"Yes, miz. I'm not surprised. It's an—interesting sensation. I guess you get used to it, though."

"It's great fun," the girl-Guest said, turning the flitter around. "Where to, Bivouac Area Charlie?"

"Yes, miz, Bivouac Charlie it is, thank you."

"You can keep calling me 'miz' if you want to, but my name is Alyssaunde," she said.

Carl mentally reviewed the Rules for conduct with Guests. The two General Regulations were to avoid physical contact if possible, and always to be polite and proper. The usual formula for politeness was calling a Guest "miz" if a female, and "sir" if a male or if you couldn't tell. If a Guest wanted to be called by her name there was no rule against it, and it was certainly more polite to do what she wished. It never occurred to Carl that the reason there was no ban on first-name calling was that the framers of the Rules had never conceived of the possibility.

"Alley-san, yes, miz."

The girl laughed again. "Alyssaunde," she corrected him, "and no 'miz.'"

Carl struggled with the unfamiliar syllables until Alyssaunde was satisfied with his pronunciation. As she guided the flitter toward Bivouac Charlie, he examined the interior and tried to make sense of what he saw. The boat was a four-seater, two bucket seats in front and two in back. The seats faced forward while the boat was moving, and large web straps held you in place; but they swiveled freely while the craft hovered. There were windows all around the body and two screens that showed what was happening underneath. All the dials and knobs were around the seat Alyssaunde was in, so whoever sat there obviously controlled what the ship did.

"Are you an officer?" the girl asked.

"No." Carl struggled between the familiar "miz" and the newly learned "Alyssaunde," and decided to try to avoid both if he could. "I'm a corporal. See the two stripes painted on the sleeves of the chain mail? One stripe would be a private and three a sergeant. Officers have epaulettes."

"Oh. Thank you."

"Would you"—he indicated the small pile of booty at his feet—"like to buy a souvenir?"

The golden laugh again. "No, thank you, soldier. What would I do with a sword or an arrow?"

"They're crossbow bolts," Carl said. "Most of the Guests want souvenirs. They're"—he searched for the word—"ethnic."

"I'm not in the market for ethnic hunks of metal, but I appreciate the offer. Have you been in the army long?"

"Over four years."

"Do you like it?"

"I guess so. I don't know much else. I'm an army brat."

"Army brat?"

"I was brought up in an army camp," Carl explained. "My father was a sergeant in the light cavalry."

"I don't suppose you spent much time in school," Alyssaunde said, "following your father from camp to camp."

"I was brought up in Bivouac Bravo, where my father's company is, and I went to the camp school for the full six years. I didn't transfer to Bivouac Charlie until after I enlisted."

"Ah!" Alyssaunde said, as though a great light had dawned. "Then the bivouac areas are stationary?"

"Of course. Why would anyone want to move a bivouac?"

There was a pause. Carl wanted to ask the Guest some questions of his own, about her, about the machine they were traveling in, about why she wanted to know so much about him; but one of the strictest Rules was to answer the Guest's questions but not to ask them any. It was permitted to ask questions of the Inspectors, but they invariably answered that it was Classified Information, and then marked your name down in their little black books. No one knew what was done with the books, but it was generally conceded that it was wise to keep your name out of the Inspectors' black books.

"I'll set you down right here," the Guest said, breaking the pause. "The bivouac's right over the hill, and it would probably be wiser for both of us if no one sees you get out of the flitter."

"Yes, miz," Carl said, gathering up his booty. "Thank you." He stepped out of the flitter and started trudging up the hill.

The flitter shot into the air and paused about five feet over his head. "Alyssaunde," said an amplified whisper in his ear. The boat darted off, and she waved a slender hand at him as it climbed. "*Alyssaunde!*" the whisper came again, and then the flitter was just a dot in the sky. And then it was gone.

❊ 3 ❊

"Now look, Jemmy," Carl said with the air of a man trying to stay calm despite extreme provocation, "have you ever tried selling a breastplate? How do you know a breastplate won't sell?"

The little man behind the counter lifted his hands toward the sky. "Look," he appealed to heaven, "now he's trying to teach me how to sell souvenirs." He waggled a finger at Carl. "Look, I don't tell you how to go out and fight your battles; you don't come back and tell me how to sell my souvenirs; agreed?"

"Whose souvenirs?"

"All right, *our* souvenirs. But a breastplate won't sell, regardless."

"Listen, Jemmy, how often do I get a chance to capture a Saracen Grand Knight? In yesterday's battle, at great risk to my own skin, I make my biggest capture in four years of active duty. Now his ransom gets split up by the whole company, but his armor is all mine. And you're my agent."

"These heavy, one-piece breastplates won't sell," Jemmy insisted. "The tourists don't want to lug anything like that around."

"I'll tell you what, Jemmy; take this one and if it doesn't sell I'll never bring you another breastplate as long as I'm on active duty."

"Deals he's making me yet," Jemmy informed whomever he was speaking to in the sky. "All right, I'll take it, but it's against my better judgment."

21

Carl turned the breastplate over and, in an inconspicuous spot on the back, pressed a rubber stamp against the leather lining. The stamp, in indelible green ink, read:

PRIZE
captured in open battle
by C. F. Allan, Corporal
Eleventh L.M.I.A.C.
Never Dishonored
AGENT: HONEST JEMMY

"There." He tossed the breastplate onto the pile of iron-mongery already on Jemmy's counter. "Add it to my list."

The little man scribbled something on the bottom of a receipt form and, tearing it off the pad, handed it to Carl. "Here you are, Carl. Look, I hope it sells. You're one of my best clients and I don't like arguing with you. Besides, I got too much trouble arguing with the customers and the Inspectors to argue with you."

"You've got Inspector trouble? What are they crabbing about now?"

"My sign." Jemmy pointed to the wooden signboard over the counter. It read: GENUINE BATTLE SOUVENIRS.

"What's wrong with the sign?"

"You like it? It's distinctive, maybe? Here, I'll show you what I wanted to put up." He fished under the counter and came up with a sheet of heavy brown paper. "This is what I wanted it to look like."

Carl examined the paper. Carefully and neatly printed on it in blunt pencil was the legend:

HONEST JEMMY'S
Authentic Battle Souvenirs
GUARANTEED GENUINE
The Best Prices in the Bivouac

"It looks OK to me. The Inspectors won't let you put it up?"

"To you it looks OK; to me it looks OK; to the Inspectors it doesn't look ethnic." He shrugged. "Ethnic yet."

"Well," Carl said, "tough luck. It would have been a good-looking sign, but you know the old saying, 'Never question the decisions of Inspectors, for they are hard nosed and quick to anger.'"

"You're right, of course. Look, come back in a week and I should have some of this stuff sold for you."

"OK. I sure hope you do; I'll be able to use the scrip." Carl shook hands with Jemmy and wandered out of the little shop onto the Street of Guests, the only street with sidewalks in the whole bivouac. Four six-foot-high beetles hopped by the store entrance, chittering among themselves. Carl stepped aside to allow the Guests to pass. Two four-foot-high decapods with small metal cylinders plugged into a slit on their backs paused to stare at Carl. Carl took a step in their direction and the thinner one shrank back toward the heavier, who put a protective tentacle around it and whistled reassuringly.

Carl circled the two at a good distance so as not to alarm them and hurried back to the tent area. He had already missed dinner, but he had some crackers and dried meat in his locker. Washed down with a crock of the beer that Tent Seven kept illegally in a lockbox in the stream, it would make an adequate meal.

Corporal deMitre, Carl's tent-mate, looked up from the chain mail he was repairing when Carl strode into the tent. "Where've you been, Allan?" he demanded. "They're looking for you."

Carl went to his locker and constructed himself a cracker and dried-meat sandwich. "Who's looking for me?" he asked. "Where's the mustard?"

"How come you only brought back one beer?" de-

Mitre asked, putting down the pliers and pushing aside the spool of wire. "This wire-twisting is tiresome work. Here's the mustard crock; I guess it's empty."

"What do you mean, you *guess* it's empty?" Carl asked, shaking his head. "You're weird, deMitre. Either it is empty or it isn't empty. And it was full yesterday when I bought it from the commissary. And if you want a beer, you can get it yourself. What'd you do with the mustard, anoint yourself?"

"Yes," deMitre said.

Carl, his mouth open, stared at deMitre. Then he waved his sandwich feebly in the air. "What?" he asked.

"Well, sort of," deMitre said. "I got this cold."

"Weird," Carl repeated.

"They told me to plaster mustard all over my chest if I got a cold," deMitre explained.

"*My* mustard?" Carl asked. "Did it work, at least?"

"You should have got the large-sized crock," deMitre said. Carl looked for something to throw, but there was nothing handy, so he ate his sandwich.

"They want to see you, seven o'clock," deMitre told him, going back to his pliers and spool of wire. "What you done now?"

"Who wants to see me?" Carl asked patiently.

"Higgins. At seven o'clock."

"Captain-Chevalier Higgins? What for?"

"That's what I asked you," deMitre said placidly.

Carl munched on his sandwich and stared reflectively at the canvas ceiling. It couldn't be anything serious, he told himself. Higgins would have sent a couple of guards for him if it were anything serious; Higgins didn't fool around. But it didn't have to be that serious—not serious enough to arrest him, just serious enough to break him back down to trooper. There was all the little stuff, of course: things that were technically illegal but winked at by the brass.

Like the bottle of beer he was drinking, Carl realized. "Here," he said, handing the bottle to deMitre, "I don't want any more. Finish it."

"Well," deMitre said, taking the bottle, "if you insist."

Carl snorted and checked his watch. "Time for evening exercises," he said. "You coming?"

"I gave my platoon the night off," deMitre said. "They're in good shape, and I don't want to over-exercise them. It takes the edge off."

Carl shook his head, wonderingly. "One of these days you're going to get in serious trouble, you know that?" he said. "You bend or twist regulations a little, you get away with it for a while; but you start breaking them, or eliminating them, and you'll have a noble finger ripping off your chevrons."

"*I'm* not the one going to see Higgins," deMitre reminded him.

Carl left the tent without replying and went over to his corner of the parade field, where his platoon was stripped down to their kilts waiting for him. They had a roughhouse game of kickball going, which died out as he approached. They were good men, Carl reflected, the best. And he was lucky to be their platoon leader. Their tight discipline in battle and their sharp appearance on the parade field made Carl look good as their leader. They were a well-behaved group, too; getting in trouble just often enough so there could be no doubt about their masculinity, but not enough so that the discipline officer would remember any of their names.

"Fall in!" Carl called, reaching his assigned spot on the grass. The fourteen men in his platoon fell in to a single line, in size order, shortest to the right, and lined up.

"Ten-shun!" Carl called, when the fidgeting lessened. The men snapped to positions of attention, freezing in place, ramrod stiff. They seemed to be slanting slightly to the left, but Carl decided to ignore that. "Trooper Bitter," he called, "come out and lead the platoon." Carl believed in giving each of the men practice at command. It was, after all, the only way of finding out which of them had the potential for leadership.

"Yessir, Corporal," Bitter replied, double-timing out to the front of the platoon.

Carl removed himself to the side of the platoon and joined in the exercises as Trooper Bitter led the men in the Daily Decade. Carl performed the motions by rote, allowing his mind to concentrate on worrying about why Higgins wanted to see him. After the exercises Carl delivered the obligatory "Inspirational Talk," this evening a ten-minute dissertation on the value of keeping one's chain mail shiny, including the dubious proposition that it would tend to blind the enemy in battle. His father, Field Sergeant Frederic ben Shahn Allan, Retired, had taught him that, having himself been blinded by a dazzling helm and losing the last two fingers of his left hand as a direct result.

Then it was seven o'clock, and Carl had an appointment with Captain-Chevalier Higgins. He dismissed his troop and headed for the command tent. Carl wondered, as he approached the tent, why the two-story, wood-frame building was called a "tent." He wondered about a lot of the customs that, sanctified by ancient usage, no longer had any actual meaning or relevance. Why did their inspection kits contain twelve tent pegs, although their tents were framed with two-by-fours and had concrete floors? Why were they supposed to ignore the presence of Guests at some times, like during battles or ceremonies, and politely acknowledge them at others, like on the Street of Guests? Why were there some things that were just never talked about, like what was on the other side of the barrier? What did Captain-Chevalier Higgins want to see him about?

TOMORROW KNIGHT 27

Well, the last he was about to find out. Carl walked through the orderly room and, tucking his knit cap under his arm, knocked on the commander's door.

"Come in!"

Carl entered, took three paces forward, snapped to attention, and saluted. Then the feeling of shock hit the pit of his stomach, as he saw who else was in the room.

Captain-Chevalier Higgins was behind the desk.

On the observers' platform were seven Guests: a pair of beetle Guests; an improbable-looking creature with three legs and a tall eye-stalk; three squat, pug-faced, lion-maned, massively muscled types that smelled vaguely of methane; and the girl Guest, Alyssaunde. *Alyssaunde!*

To Captain-Chevalier Higgins' right were two aides-de-camp of staff rank and His Most Righteous and Honorable Majesty, Hiram VI, by the grace of God King of the Celts and Picts and Jutes, Emperor of Rome-in-Exile, and Hereditary Foe of the Supremacy of Allah. His Majesty was commonly known as Hiram, King of the West, as his traditional enemy was called Boris, Emir of the East; this showing their positions as rulers respectively of the west and east halves of Sector Seven.

Hiram VI was smiling, Carl noted, while Captain-Chevalier Higgins was frowning. The aides were maintaining a discreet neutrality. The Guests—how could you tell? Except for the girl, Alyssaunde. But Carl couldn't—mustn't—think of her as a girl: she was a Guest. Whether she looked horrible or beautiful, she was a Guest, and not a person.

Carl kept his gaze straight ahead and held his salute until Capain-Chevalier Higgins returned it. "Lance Corporal Allan reporting as directed, sir."

"At ease, Corporal," Higgins said. "You know why you're here, of course."

"No, sir," Carl said, fighting a sudden impulse to scream. It was clear that everyone else in the room knew why he was there.

"Pah!" His Majesty Hiram VI suddenly spoke up. "We have no need of all this ceremony. *I* certainly have no need of any ceremony. I'm sure Corporal Allan would rather do without the ceremony; isn't that so, Corporal?"

"Yes, Your Majesty," Carl assured Hiram VI. "No ceremony would suit me fine, Your Majesty."

"Right," Hiram VI agreed. "Kneel."

"What? That is, excuse me, Your Majesty."

"Kneel down, boy. You're about to become a knight-brevet." He strode to the center of the room, in front of Carl, and pulled out his great sword.

Carl gulped. Then he took a deep breath. It had never occurred to him that sometimes *good* things happen when one is ordered to report to one's commander. Carl found that he was still holding his breath, and he released it in a short gasp. He kneeled.

Hiram VI took his sword in both hands and applied the flat of it to Carl's left shoulder, and then his right. "By the power vested in me by my hereditary position, and the Ruling Council, and in recognition of the great and courageous act of heroism committed by Carl Frederic Allan of the Eleventh—Eleventh?— that's right, Eleventh Light Mounted Infantry Attack Company in the recent battle against the Horde of Allah in coming to the defense of his sovereign against overwhelming odds—I never did thank you for that, boy—as reported to the awards committee by Guest and observer c'Chank'k'k Rgh'hagh't"—here Hiram nodded to the taller beetle, who shyly waved a mandible—"I hereby and herewith give and grant to the aforesaid Carl Frederic Allan, my loyal subject, a grant and patent of arms and a brevet to the rank of knight-cadet."

Hiram VI paused here, and took a deep breath, then he sheathed his sword and took Carl by the hand. "Rise, Sir Knight," he said in his most deep, resonant, ceremonial, commanding voice.

❋ 4 ❋

Carl went to bed late that night; it must have been almost ten o'clock by the time he crawled into his bedroll. He had much to think about, and he spent the time sitting on the bench outside his tent, staring into the darkness, and thinking. First there was the problem of what device to pick for his arms. He would have to consult with his father on that. His father would be delighted and proud when he heard the news, and would probably spend a couple of months researching family history to come up with a unique and appropriate device for Carl Frederic. It would be a blessing for the old man; give him something of legitimate importance to do. Since Frederic ben Shahn had accepted retirement four years ago, he hadn't been able to find anything that interested him to keep himself busy. He was still a young man, too, not yet fifty, with an awful lot of boredom to look forward to unless he found something to do with his time. The fighting arm of the Holy Crusade used up men young, and few of them could adapt themselves to civilian life when they unstrapped and hung up the sword and buckler.

This fate of his father's was one that no longer directly concerned Carl. Knights did not retire. And the step from knight-brevet to knight was a sure one, if sometimes it did take years. Carl would be notified at some future time, by one of the army's mysterious internal processes, that he had been accepted at one of

TOMORROW KNIGHT

the officers' candidate schools run by the army (or possibly the navy, even though Carl had never even seen the ocean).

When Carl had successfully graduated from the candidate school, he would be nominated for one of the orders of knighthood by his sponsor. And since said sponsor was Hiram VI himself, Carl surely would be accepted. Then he would be Lieutenant-Chevalier Allan; or possibly Lieutenant-Bath, or Lieutenant-Garter, or even Lieutenant-Roundtable Allan. Hiram VI himself was a hereditary Knight of the Round Table.

Knights were also not limited by the barrier the way commoners were. They were open to be assigned to other sectors if there was need of them there, or if there were too many in their home sector. The few vague tales Carl had heard of the world beyond Sector Seven were the retellings of stories told by garrulous old knights who had spent part of their service in other sectors before retiring and coming home. Stories of whole battles fought with guns, like the fowling pieces the nobility used, but able to reload much more quickly, or, in some versions, to fire several shots before reloading. Stories of vehicles that traveled at great speed along the ground without horses; and other vehicles, used by men and not Guests, that flew through the air supported by great metal wings. Stories of tall buildings with moving rooms that took you from one floor to the next. Carl went to sleep remembering these wonderful, mythical stories.

When Carl woke up it was the middle of the night, and his mind was full of visions of Alyssaunde, the soft, gentle lady who rustled when she moved and smelled like—Carl had no words to describe her smell, but could only try to recapture the memory of it. He tried to roll over and go back to sleep, but the image of this girl who could handle a flitterboat as if it were something alive kept pushing up from his subconscious. He wanted to think about Alyssaunde. He wanted to dream about Alyssaunde, but in the waking, musing daydreams with which a man thinks about a woman, not in the deep sleep, unremembered dreams of the subconscious.

Carl slid out of his bedroll and pulled his boots on. Being careful not to wake deMitre—not that there was any known way to wake deMitre before his full eight hours—he left the tent. Both moons had risen now, and the ground glowed with that peculiar shadowless light that makes the background brooding and the foreground a series of misshapen lumps that cannot be identified without prior knowledge.

A flitterboat passed overhead, and Carl felt a momentary twinge of fear. It was an Inspector coming to get him for the way he was thinking about a Guest. Then he realized how foolish that was. If the Inspectors could monitor their thinking, then Carl and most of his friends in the bivouac would have been taken away long ago. No, the twinge was from Carl's own guilt feelings. The years of schooling and indoctrination were not to be eliminated so lightly. A Guest was a Guest was a Guest, and regardless of shape or size or smell was to be treated by the Rules of Conduct. Which didn't include fraternizing. Carl realized that he was obviously going to continue thinking about Alyssaunde, so he and his conscience would just have to fight it out.

Another flitterboat passed, obscuring the Little Moon for an instant. Carl walked toward the parade ground, staring at the Little Moon low on the horizon in front of him. The Little Moon, a small, bright sphere, much brighter than the moon, moved across the sky so fast that you could almost see it moving. It would rise and set twice in the same night. Carl stared at it and thought about Earth, and about the other planets he would never get to see. The Guests came from other planets, he knew. Not from the moon, or the Little Moon, but from planets so far that they circled stars that were faint dots in Earth's night sky. Alyssaunde was a Guest, and she probably came from one of those distant dots. And she would probably go back after a brief stay on Earth. And Carl would never see her again.

Carl reached the parade field, and a flitterboat lifted into the air as if startled by his presence. There seemed to be a lot of them around tonight, which was unusual; there was nothing to see after dark, so the flitters usually went back to wherever they came from. Maybe Alyssaunde was up there in the dark sky, in one of the hovering flitterboats.

Then all at once, as Carl stared wistfully at the hovering flitterboats in the dark sky, the connecting facts popped out of his subconscious and Carl *knew* why the flitterboats were there.

They were waiting for an attack.

Somewhere out there in the dark the Saracen Horde was gathered for a night attack on the Holy Crusade. The Guests always knew in advance of even the most secret surprise attack, and the flitterboats always gathered around the site even before the battle started. How they knew was beyond Carl's knowledge, but know they did.

And now Carl knew. The Saracens were out there in the dark beyond the sentry posts. Probably watching him right now, Carl thought, feeling a prickly sensation along the base of his spine. He tried to act casual, just continuing along with what he was doing. What had he been doing? He tried to remember. Thinking, that's what. How does one manage to look as if he is merely thinking?

Doing his best to keep thinking, Carl started back for the tent area. He shook his tent-mate awake first when he arrived.

deMitre choked, gurgled, then swung blindly at Carl. His fist connected with the tent pole. "Blast!" he screamed. "What under the two moons are you doing, Allan? It *is* you, Allan, isn't it?"

"Shut up," Carl Frederic told him. "Get dressed, or at least get your boots on."

"Why the hell should I do that?" deMitre demanded. "It must be three o'clock in the morning."

"We're under attack," Carl told him. "Or we will be any minute now. Get dressed and wake the rest of the troop. I've got to go tell the O.D. and Captain Higgins."

deMitre sat up in his bedroll and scratched his head. "Let's see if I've got this right," he said. "We're being attacked, and nobody knows about it but you."

"Something like that," Carl admitted.

"I think this brevet stuff has gone to your head," deMitre told him. "You planning to bull your way to Grand General before you're thirty, are you?"

Carl grinned. "You better hope I don't get you in my company, or you won't sleep through the evening calisthentics."

"Your company!" deMitre snorted, pulling his pants on. "Your corps, more likely. I look forward to being a humble platoon leader in Allan's Army."

Carl slid his chain-mail vest on over his head and buckled on his short sword. "I'm heading for the command tent," he said. "Wake up your platoon and mine and send scouts over to the other platoon leaders. Earth knows how long we've got."

"This attack of yours had better happen, that's all I've got to say," deMitre grumbled, pulling on his own armor.

"My," Carl said, "you are a bloodthirsty lad, aren't you?" And with that he left the tent and dogtrotted over to the command tent. All deliberate speed, but without actually running. If the Saracens were in a position to watch, a dogtrotting trooper could be a late guard; a running trooper might know something.

Carl couldn't take a chance on precipitating the attack.

The Charge of Quarters, a skinny trooper named Stout, was mopping the orderly-room floor when Carl burst in. "Watch it!" he yelled. "Don't get your muddy bootprints in here or I'll have to mop it all over again."

"Not tonight, you won't," Carl Frederic said. "Who's the Officer of the Day?"

"Lieutenant Von Strasse. He's asleep in the office."

"I'll go wake him up. You go wake up the other platoon leaders and tell them to rouse their men."

"Yes, Corporal," Stout said, dropping his mop and heading for the door. He stopped just short of it and turned around. "Ah, Corporal, why am I waking them? I mean, they're sure to ask."

"Tell them we're about to be attacked by Saracens, that should satisfy them."

"Right," Stout said. He started out the door, then turned back and buckled on his sword and put his helmet over his service cap. Then he raced out.

Carl Frederic shook Lieutenant Von Strasse awake. "Under attack?" the lieutenant said, rubbing his eyes. "What makes you think that?"

The high-pitched whine of a Saracen war-horn blasted in through the open window, sounding the attack from somewhere close by. Somewhere, Carl thought, much too close by.

"I see," Lieutenant Von Strasse said. "You've made your point. How many are awake?"

"Twenty or thirty by now," Carl said. "I hope."

"I also," the lieutenant agreed. "Well, let's get out there."

They ran out into the night, swords drawn, the lieutenant in his stockinged feet. The sudden dark, after even the dim light of the gas lamp in the orderly room, blinded Carl. He should have remembered that, he thought, and kept one eye closed while inside.

Now it would take a few minutes for his night vision to come back, and almost a full half hour before it returned completely.

"Can't see or hear a thing," Lieutenant Von Strasse whispered to Carl. "What's happening?"

"They're out there somewhere," Carl said.

"I imagine attacking in the dark is a somewhat slow process," Lieutenant Von Strasse commented. "Although with both moons out you should be able to see pretty well once your eyes are adjusted. We have to do something about getting red lenses to put over the orderly-room lamp."

"What are your orders, sir?" Carl asked.

"Ah, yes, my orders," Lieutenant Von Strasse mused.

Someone cursed in the distance. Steel struck steel somewhere close by. There was a wild scream and a crashing sound. The battle had begun.

"Perhaps we'd better wake up Captain-Chevalier Higgins, sir," Carl suggested.

"Captain-Chevalier Higgins is spending the night at Castle Elsinore, as a guest of His Majesty," the lieutenant said. "I guess that puts me in charge. Go to your platoon, Corporal, and . . . No; your platoon can take care of itself. Presumably they're awake, dressed, and together."

"I think so, sir."

"Well, the Saracens are here only to take prisoners. Anyone still in his tent is their meat. Make it from tent to tent and order the men to scatter and hide and only fight if they're cornered. I'll send a runner to the Twenty-Seventh, and they should be able to form up and get their asses over here within half an hour."

"The men won't like running away from the enemy, sir," Carl said.

"It's not running away," Lieutenant Von Strasse said. "It's keeping out of sight and letting the enemy tire themselves out thrashing away at empty tents.

The Saracens will be methodically going from tent to tent. There's no way platoons that aren't already awake and together, like yours, can group. They'll either get killed or captured if they fight individually. The company fund can't afford to pay the ransoms if too many of the men get captured." Von Strasse sounded annoyed. "Why this had to happen while I was O.D. and Higgins was away is what I want to know."

"I'll get on it right away, sir," Carl said, giving a perfunctory salute which the lieutenant returned. He was beginning to be able to see again.

"Very good," Von Strasse said. "Hell, they've probably captured twenty percent of the men already. There goes Captain-Chevalier Higgins' plans for a new mess hall." With his sword clutched grimly in his hand, he turned and stalked off toward the nearest sounds of battle.

Carl obeyed orders and went from tent to tent telling the men not to try to form up but to split for the high ground. Many had done this already. A few were still asleep, despite the noise of impending battle, and Carl had to kick them awake. Several were crouched, dressed, and hiding in their tents, and almost skewered Carl as he entered.

The noise of the fighting approached, and Carl decided it was time to follow the orders he was transmitting. Off to the left was a thick wooded area where it would be easy to avoid a fight. He headed toward it until a large mound blocked his path. The mound turned at his approach, and the double moons revealed it as one of the largest Saracen troopers Carl had ever seen.

"Excuse me," Carl said, trying to duck under the Saracen's upraised arm.

The Saracen growled and lunged, bringing his sword arm around and clubbing downward with the pommel of his broadsword. The move grazed Carl's shoulder as he butted upward, mashing the smooth top of his helmet square against the Saracen's chin. The Saracen stumbled backward and sat heavily, blood spurting from the corner of his mouth. He put his hand to his mouth and then held it away, examining the bloodstained fingers with interest. "I cut my tongue," he said wonderingly.

"Yield!" Carl commanded, holding his sword to the Saracen's chest.

"You son of an uncircumcised pig!" the Saracen shouted, slapping Carl's sword aside and springing to his feet. "I cut my tongue! You made me bleed! I'm going to get you for that!" He took his broadsword in both hands and, with a savage roar, lumbered toward Carl.

Carl retreated rapidly in the direction of the wood, mindful of his lieutenant's orders not to engage in a fight if he could help it. And if he could help it, he would gladly not fight this monster Saracen. Once he became a knight he might have to fight to defend his honor, but everyone knew that troopers had no honor.

He passed the first tree two steps ahead of the Saracen. Now he was in the wood, and the thick branches filtered out the light of the two moons, and it was pitch dark. Carl turned left, tripped, and fell heavily. The Saracen, cursing loudly, stumbled on past him and into the depths of the wood.

Carl pulled himself to his feet and continued on in the direction he was headed. In a few minutes he was thoroughly lost. The screaming and clanking sounds of battle were his only orientation, and they seemed to come from all around. He kept walking. In a little while the sound was isolated, and he could tell it was coming from behind him and to the left.

It was probably about time to get back to the unit and join in the fighting. The Twenty-Seventh Light Mounted Infantry Attack Company, the Eleventh's neighbors, should be ready to counterattack, and Carl Frederic should try to locate and regroup his men. He struck off through the trees and kept heading in a line that should take him out of the wood. In a little while the battle sounds were coming from behind him and to the right. Either the battle had moved considerably in the past few minutes, or Carl was going in a circle.

Carl paused to reason out his problem. The answer seemed to be to travel by sound rather than sight, as long as he couldn't see anything. He started out again, trying to keep the noise of battle to his left. In a few minutes he was back out of the trees.

"Halt!" a shadowy figure in front of him demanded. "Advance and give the countersign."

Carl tried to remember the countersign. Surely he must have been told the countersign. It all seemed so long ago. "Beachball," he said.

"Good guess," the shadowy figure advised him. "Want to try again?"

"It *sounded* like 'beachball,'" Carl complained. "Dromedary?"

The guard poked a twelve-foot pike at him. "Down on your face," he said. "Don't cause any trouble."

"I never argue with the legally constituted chain of command," Carl said. "An order from a guard on duty is as a command from the Emperor." He fell forward, landing flat on his face, and remained there.

A flitterboat passed low over their heads.

"Good thinking," the guard said, coming forward to examine Carl from close up. "Say, aren't you Corporal Allan from the Eleventh?"

"That's right," Carl said, twisting his head to look up at the guard. "Isn't this the Eleventh?"

"No, the Eleventh is over that way, where all the noise is coming from. This is the Nineteenth. What are you doing way over here?"

"I got lost," Carl told him. "The Saracens have attacked us. Don't you people know that?"

"Of course," the trooper told him. "The captain has doubled the guard."

"Oh," Carl said. "Well, if you'll let me up now that you recognize me, I guess I'll head back to my unit."

The trooper stepped back and raised his pike to present arms. "Only doing my job, Corporal," he said.

"I wouldn't have it any other way," Carl assured him, climbing to his feet. "Carry on, trooper." He gave a halfhearted salute, and started toward the battle noise. The screaming sounded louder and more organized: the counterattack had probably begun. Carl Frederic's place was with his platoon.

He had gone no more than a couple of hundred yards when the four of them jumped him. Four Saracen troopers; they had been quietly sitting out the battle by the side of a large rock when Carl blundered into their midst. He was not only an enemy in their eyes, he was a corporal who had seen them goofing off. He might report them after the battle—if he lived to tell about it.

They leaped without warning, as though pulled by a common string. Carl had barely time to get his sword up before they were upon him. He parried all their blows and retreated before them, carefully not letting any of them get behind him. It took him over a minute to maneuver around and get his back to the rock so he could keep them all in sight before him.

The four Saracens were young, inexperienced troopers, no match for Carl in single combat. But there were four of them, and if they just kept bashing long enough one of them would get through Carl's guard. Or they would tire him out to the point where he couldn't keep his guard up anymore.

Carl kept them far enough away with the point of his sword so that they had to use full arm swings or lunges to get through his guard. Full arm swings were difficult with four of them facing him, as they kept getting in each other's way; and they were reluctant to try lunges, as that would bring their bodies entirely too close to that sharp point on the end of Carl's sword. So they stood their distance and hacked away at him, waiting to tire him out and finish him.

Carl could feel himself tiring, and the muscles of his shoulder began to ache. He knew that he'd better do something, and do it fast. Every second that passed was further sapping his strength. Trying to break away from the four Saracens would be risky, but staying and fighting them was eventual death.

The Saracens were coming in two at a time, the other two staying just out of range, and switching every minute or so to rest. Carl backed along the face of the rock, causing the two in front to clump closer together, then made his break. Instead of breaking away from them, where the other two in the rear were waiting for him, he broke toward them. With a sudden sweep of his sword he knocked the other two aside; then he lunged toward the point dead center between them.

They were knocked aside, and one of them stumbled. Carl carefully kicked him as he went down, and slashed waist-high at the other's side. Then he swiveled to face the other two men, his sword at ready.

A flitterboat swooped down to get a better view of the action.

The first two men were out of the fight: one rolling on the ground clutching his abdomen, and the second sitting quietly by the rock and keeping both hands on the pressure points that would lessen the flow of blood through the long gash in his side right below the chain shirt. The other two men were warily approaching Carl, who was backing away from them, trying for a clear shot at escaping into the woods. They were not going to underestimate him again, and had already tired him out to the point where, with care, they could take him.

Carl switched his sword to his left hand to rest his right, and concentrated on parrying the renewed attack. The two Sarcens were getting practice in keeping out of each other's way, and pressed in on each side of Carl, methodically hacking away to get by his guard. Soon they would succeed.

Carl gathered himself for a lunge—one mad make-or-break dash into the wood. In a few seconds either he would be among the trees and away, or he would be dead.

Suddenly, as Carl smashed the two blades aside and leaped forward, a searingly bright white light flashed on and impaled him in its beam, blinding him. He tripped and fell flat on his face. Something solid cracked into the back of his head.

❋ 5 ❋

It was some time before Carl came to. The sun had risen and was already well up in the sky, Carl realized, staring out the window of the flitterboat.

The *flitterboat?*

With a groan, Carl tried to push himself up to a sitting position. The girl in the command chair hurried over to him when she heard the noise. It was Alyssaunde, Carl noticed blurrily, then he collapsed back in the couch and lost consciousness again.

When he came around again it was dusk, and Alyssaunde was sitting by the couch looking down at him. "Hello," she said softly when she saw his eyes open.

He focused on her face and thought about this for some time. Finally he figured out what she had said and what he should do about it. "Hello," he replied. His voice seemed to come from far away, and his tongue was unnaturally thick. There was something wrong about where he was and what was happening to him, but he couldn't figure it out now. He closed his eyes and went back to sleep.

This time he slept for only a short while, and when he woke Alyssaunde fed him hot soup from a fine porcelain cup. Neither of them spoke. Carl finished the soup and Alyssaunde removed the cup and then patted an alcohol-dampened cloth across his face.

"What happened?" Carl asked. He tried to sit up again and found that he couldn't. He was trussed up like a mummy from his waist to right below his arms.

His left arm was bandaged from elbow to shoulder, and his head was wrapped in what seemed like yards of bandage. He felt very weak, and the effort of trying to move made him dizzy.

"What do you remember?" Alyssaunde asked, sitting next to him and staring into his eyes.

Having Alyssaunde that close made him uncomfortable, and it wasn't just because she was a Guest. He closed his eyes and reached for the elusive memory of his recent past. "I was fighting off a couple of Saracens," Carl remembered. "I was just about to make a dive for the cover of a nearby grove of trees when some idiot blinded me with a bright light. I've never seen a light that bright. Then someone clobbered me over the back of the head. It must have been one of the two Saracens. Then I woke up here. Since they were trying to kill me, this must be heaven. And you—"

"Not quite," Alyssaunde told him. As a matter of fact, if you promise not to yell, or try to strangle me, there's something I should tell you." She looked faintly amused.

"What's that?" Carl asked.

"I was the idiot," Alyssaunde said. She shook her head slowly. "It was inexcusable, and I'm more sorry than you can imagine. I wouldn't want to hurt any of you people."

"You turned on the light? What for? Then it must have been you in the flitterboat over our heads." Carl struggled to sit up, and this time he made it. "Whatever did you turn on that light for?"

"I guess I owe you an explanation," Alyssaunde said, "seeing as I almost killed you. It was sheer stupidity. I admit it, *I* was stupid. Thoughtless and stupid. My father keeps telling me I shouldn't try to do anything that requires intelligence. Leave that to the men, he says. Maybe he's right."

"In my experience," Carl said slowly, thinking over

each word before it came out, "the women are, if anything, smarter than the men. Women get better grades in school. All the teachers are women. Why, I knew a girl once who used to read; I mean, for fun. She would just sit there and read a book for fun. She was pretty smart, that girl."

"Is that right?" Alyssaunde sounded interested. "Perhaps in your society, primitive as it is, women are allowed to reach their full potential. In mine women are regarded as objects: playthings for the men. Be pretty or die, or at least join a nunnery, that's what you're—we're—taught."

"Really?" Carl said. "Well, you sure are pretty!" Then he turned red. "I'm sorry, I shouldn't have said that."

Alyssaunde smiled again. "Why not? It's true," she said, but not as if she were proud of the fact or regarded it as much of an accomplishment. "It's not hard, you know. Just start out with a decent body, eat properly when you're growing up, and spend ten years learning the cosmetic arts. It helps to have money. Malnutrition is just hell on a girl's figure."

"Why'd you turn the light on?" Carl asked, as much to change the subject as for any other reason. After all, if a Guest wanted to use a spotlight, it was not forbidden. Guests were not supposed to interfere, but throwing a light on an existing battle would probably not be regarded as interference. Spotlighting a group waiting in ambush would be interfering, probably, but even then an Inspector would have to have seen it to make the complaint. Citizens were not to question the actions of Guests.

"I was trying to take pictures," Alyssaunde said. "I'm doing a photo-essay on some aspects of your culture. I meant to take them in infrared light, but the selector switch was incorrectly set." She shook her head. "See how you can do that without even thinking about it? Here I am trying to blame the switch, which is a mindless mechanical device and merely stays where I set it. *I* set it wrongly. Me. It's my fault. I'm sorry and I apologize. The switch is not sorry."

Carl didn't follow any of this. He decided it was because he was so weak. "Where are we?" he asked. "What time is it?"

"It's about nine in the evening," Alyssaunde told him. "The day after your fight. That is, actually, the same day, since the battle began well after midnight. You know what I mean. We're sitting on top of one of the Altoona Mounds."

"But they're off limits," Carl said.

"Not to me," Alyssaunde told him. "Someday I plan to dig them up and get a glimpse of the ancient city they say is buried here."

"Oh," Carl said. "Is that what it is?" He was beginning to feel stronger and his head was clearing. He raised his arms and twisted his body experimentally to judge the extent of the damage. "Well, I guess I haven't bought my ticket," he said. "Who packaged me?"

"Ticket?" Alyssaunde said. "Packaged?"

"Who packaged me—who wrapped me up?"

"Bandaged you. I did. What about a ticket?"

"I said I guess I haven't bought my ticket. That's what we call it when we're retired and put on half-pay because of honorable wounds. They give you a card to carry around saying you're honorably retired and can shop in the commissary and eat at the mess and like that. It's called a ticket; so getting disabling wounds is called buying your ticket. It's just the way we talk. You packaged me? You sure did a good job; where'd you learn?"

"It's amazing how quickly the different ethno-cultures develop their own argots despite all our efforts to keep the language standardized," Alyssaunde said. "I really find your idiom charming."

"Look," Carl said, "I guess you'd better put me

down somewhere. Not that I'm not grateful to you; I am. You saved my life. But I'm not supposed to be flying around in a flitterboat. I could get in a lot of trouble."

"That's true," the girl admitted. "Don't the restrictions that you must live your life by ever gall you? Don't you find them unfair?"

"I never thought about it," Carl said.

"I find the restrictions in my life very unfair," Alyssaunde said, "and there are far fewer of them for me than for you."

"I imagine," Carl said politely. He found this girl very puzzling. She was an Earther, he was sure of that by now, but she rode in a flitterboat. She talked about fairness and unfairness, but she came in low to get good pictures of Carl being hacked apart. Then, to compound the puzzle, she saved his life and packaged (bandaged?) him.

"I'll find a quiet, deserted place to let you out," Alyssaunde said. "Do you think you're strong enough to walk back to the bivouac?"

"I don't know if I'm even strong enough to stand up," Carl said, "but I guess I'll have to. Listen, miz, I do thank you very much for saving my life, even if it was your fault about the light."

"Look, you," the girl said angrily, "if I wish to chastise myself about my actions, that's my business. For you to do so is impolite, gross, vulgar, and altogether insulting. I may offer an apology, my man, but it is not your place to suggest that one is due you. Let us not forget our stations, you and me." She hit the control stick savagely, and the flitter bobbed up a couple of hundred feet.

The sudden surge threw Carl back in his couch. He felt a void in the pit of his stomach, which was immediately filled by a powerful urge to be sick. He rolled over to face the window, but the sight of the ground receding only made him feel sicker. He gulped and held his stomach.

Alyssaunde punched the course in the control board and turned back to Carl Frederic, prepared to continue the tirade. But the sight of his face was enough to make her change her mind. "What's the matter?" she said.

Carl shook his head weakly.

"It's the acceleration," Alyssaunde said. "I should have known. What a stupid thing to do; I'm sorry."

Carl smiled sickly. "That's not for me to say," he gasped, rolling over to look at her.

Alyssaunde opened a cabinet behind her and selected a small box from inside. She removed a plastic tab and broke it open, shaking the two pills it contained into Carl's hand. "Take," she directed. She handed him a small cup of water. "Drink."

Carl swallowed the pills without argument. "Thank you, miz," he said, handing her back the cup.

"I can't drop you out of sight of the bivouac," Alyssaunde said, "you'd never make it back. And I sure can't drop you anywhere in sight of the bivouac. We both share that restriction, from opposite sides of the fence. And I can't keep you here; I have to be back tonight." She drummed her fingers on the top of the control panel. "Stupid, stupid, stupid!" she said.

"Just drop me anywhere away from the bivouac," Carl said. "I'll be all right."

"Look, you," Alyssaunde said, "I didn't save your life just to leave you to bleed to death out on some rock. There's got to be— Of course!" She slapped her hands together. "Stupid! It's all in point-of-view, and I was looking through the wrong one. Of course I'll drop you. And then, like any other Guest, I'll just wander over to the bivouac and mention seeing you out there. As if I were curious to watch them pick you up and carry you back. It's all very simple when you're keeping to the right frame of reference."

"That sounds good," Carl said, thinking it over.

"Can you make it up here to the observer's seat?" Alyssaunde asked. "It would help if you picked the location to drop you."

"I think so," Carl said, pushing himself to his feet and staggering forward. The interesting thing about being so weak, Carl noticed, was that even the simplest actions became tremendous projects. He found himself as innately pleased with his success in standing up as he would have been when well with completing a complex defense pattern with the two-handed broadsword. With a sigh of accomplishment, he dropped into the right-hand observer's seat and stared through the glass at the ground below.

They were flying over a great, cubic building that stood alone in a cleared field. "We're not in your sector yet," Alyssaunde said.

"I thought not," Carl said. "That box below is nothing I recognize."

Alyssaunde peered down. "That's the Blockhouse," she told Carl.

"A good name," Carl agreed.

"It's Prime Area Government House," she explained. "The Blockhouse is its nickname."

"Prime Area?" Carl asked.

"Earth is divided into twelve areas," Alyssaunde told him. "Didn't they teach you any geography at school?"

"No," Carl said.

"Oh. Well, it is. Earth, I mean. And the Outlands. That's anyplace that isn't in one of the twelve areas. Your sector, Sector Seven, is in Prime Area."

"What does that mean?" Carl asked.

Alyssaunde shrugged. "The first, I suppose. Just in numbering order; it's not more important or anything. It just happens to be Area Number One on the maps. You know about the governors?"

"No," Carl said.

50   *Michael Kurland*

"Each area has a governor. Earth has a governor-general. They administer the planet."

"They can boss the King around; and the Emir?"

"They appointed them," Alyssaunde said.

"But Hiram the Sixth is hereditary monarch," Carl Frederic said.

"That's right," Alyssaunde said. "The Governing Council appoints all the hereditary monarchs."

"But—" Carl said.

"It's very complex," Alyssaunde said, "and you're probably not supposed to know all this stuff anyway. You're in a state of benign ignorance. Maybe if I get a chance I'll come back and explain it all to you."

"That would be nice," said Carl, who was just beginning to realize how much he didn't know.

"We've crossed," Alyssaunde said, watching some instrument on her control panel.

"What's that?" Carl asked.

Alyssaunde pointed to a glowing readout that read: 01:07:A/9. "That's the locator," she said. "It reads: Area One, Sector Seven, grid coordinates A-stroke-nine."

"Oh," Carl said.

"Your bivouac is B-stroke-seven," Alyssaunde said. "We'll be there in a couple of minutes. I'll put you down three or four miles from camp. Pick a site."

"Three miles is a long way to ask a stretcher team to carry someone," Carl said. "Couldn't we come in closer?"

"If you know a good site that will be deserted," Alyssaunde said. "Just direct me in."

The last glow of the setting sun was just fading out to the left. The Little Moon was already visible, racing across the sky, now almost directly overhead. The long shadows were dissolving into each other and all below was turning black.

"I can't see," Carl said.

Alyssaunde reached forward with one slender forefinger and tapped two buttons on her control panel. "Look through the view-glass," she said.

Carl was about to ask where the view-glass was when the question became unnecessary. One large rectangular section of the glass window between the seats had become different from the surrounding glass. Through it the ground below now looked brightly visible, almost shiny, although the colors seemed to have been shifted toward the red. The rest of the glass still showed the same old dark landscape.

"How does that work?" Carl asked.

"That's what I meant to do when I blinded you last night," Alyssaunde told him. "A pair of ultraviolet spotlights are illuminating the ground below. Of course you can't see ultraviolet. That view-glass changes the ultraviolet to light in the visible spectrum."

The only trouble with the explanation, Carl decided, was that he didn't understand any of the key words. Ultraviolet? Spectrum? But that would wait. Alyssaunde seemed to enjoy explaining things to him, even if she did do it with the air of one talking to a dull four-year-old. It wasn't his fault he didn't know any of this stuff. You can't learn something you don't know exists. He busied himself staring through the view-glass and trying to decide where to have her let him off.

"Over there," Carl said after a few minutes. "On the far side of that ridge of rocks. It's the perfect place. No one ever goes up there, but there's a path that goes right by down at the base. While you go back to the bivouac I'll climb down and meet them at the bottom by the path."

"You'll do no such thing!" Alyssaunde insisted. "You don't seem to understand how cut up you are. Any amount of exertion will open those cuts again and you'll bleed to death before they can get to you."

"You make a good case," Carl told her. "OK, I'll sit quietly and let them climb over and get me."

"That's good," Alyssaunde said. She carefully piloted the flittercraft over the rock ridge and set it down at a clear space on the far side. "Between the rocks and the trees," she said, "it's hard to find a place to set down."

Carl surveyed the thick woods surrounding them on three sides and the wall of rock on the fourth. "You did very well," he said. "The only problem is going to be explaining how I ended up here and how you happened to spot me."

"No one will think to ask," Alyssaunde assured him. "And if they do, I'll tell them that it's none of their business."

"You can do that," Carl admitted.

"You just tell them that you have no idea how you got here," Alyssaunde told Carl. "You wandered about after you were wounded."

"That's another point," Carl said. "How did I come to be, um, bandaged?"

"A good question," Alyssaunde said, resting her chin in her hands. "How indeed. You'll have to tell them you did it yourself, if they ask. Those are standard pack bandages. I believe the medication I used is, ah, unusual in your culture, but nobody will notice that."

"I did it myself," Carl agreed, staring at his carefully wrapped chest and shoulder. "I certainly did. Again I thank you, miz. You'd better let me out now."

Alyssaunde opened the port and climbed out with Carl. "Don't move around much after I leave," she said, "or the wounds may reopen."

"I'll lie here as still as any small child," Carl promised.

"Ye'll both get back into yon flying contraption," a

harsh voice behind them interrupted, "or ye'll not be going anywhere henceforth!"

They turned. Two men in foppishly brilliant costumes that Carl was unfamiliar with stood behind them. Both men pointed large-mouthed handguns of an unusual pattern at them. One of the men was very short, and the other unusually tall, but they both looked very serious.

"Hop it!" the small one directed.

❊ 6 ❊

Carl's first thought was to rush the men (after all there were only two of them), but he realized that he was probably incapable of even walking slowly over to where they were standing, much less rushing them. And he had no sword. Carl had little experience of guns, and wasn't overly afraid of them. The projectile weapons he was acquainted with were good for hitting birds with pellets at distances of up to a hundred feet, with poor accuracy, on the one out of three times they would fire at first attempt. But in his present condition the men could have merely waved the bell-shaped weapons at him and he would have been blown over by the breeze. Carl raised his hands.

"Sensible attitude," the taller man remarked. "And you, little lady?"

Alyssaunde was clearly indecisive; torn between running back into the ship, running off into the woods, or merely standing where she was and spitting at the two men. "What do you want?" she demanded, her hands on her hips.

"A little cooperation," the tall man said.

"Yer ship," the short one amended, "and yerself to drive it."

"Where'd you come from?" Carl asked. "Why are you dressed like that?"

"We'll have plenty of time to discuss such weighty matters once we are aflight," the tall man said, waving his gun around in a vague circle. "Shall we board?"

Alyssaunde, at that moment, made up her mind and dashed for the woods, her slim body low to the ground and her legs pumping furiously. *When that girl make a decision,* Carl reflected, *she goes all out.*

"Mr. O'Malley," the tall man said, "would you mind?"

"Not at all," the short man replied, and took off after Alyssaunde. He didn't look nearly as graceful when he moved, but he was all business and no wasted energy.

The tall man waved his ponderous weapon at Carl. "We have you," he observed.

"When I recover from my wounds," Carl said, "you will do me the honor of discussing this situation with me over a pair of blades."

"I doubt it," the tall man said, "but thank you for asking. Now get aboard the flitter. If the young lady eludes O'Malley, we'll have to leave as quickly as possible."

"What do you want me for?" Carl asked. "I can be of no use to you along, and can do you no damage if you leave me here."

"We need you to drive the craft," the tall man said.

Carl thought about that for a minute. Then he began to laugh. "Me?" he said. "If it were a horse I could handle it well, but I know nothing about the operation of these flitterboats."

"You conning me?" the tall man demanded.

Carl shook his head. "By the two moons," he said, "you have my word." He raised his right hand, three fingers extended, and X'd his chest with his left hand.

"By the two moons," the tall man said. "And I have a feeling that you're just the sort of boob who'd consider that a binding oath." He raised his voice and stated, "O'Malley, we need her, don't let her evade your capacious grasp."

A crashing sound answered his hail. Then a series of crashing sounds. Then silence. Then a scream.

Carl started forward, but there was nothing he could do: he was too weak, and the tall man had the gun.

The crashing noises resumed, and about half a minute later O'Malley appeared between two trees carrying Alyssaunde in both arms. Her hands were pinioned to her sides by his arms, and she was struggling and kicking her feet in a vain attempt to work loose. She was muttering something in a steady undertone, too softly for Carl to make out the words.

"She screamed?" the tall man asked, amused.

"None of it," the small man answered. "I screamed. She bit me."

The tall man laughed. "O'Malley," he said, "you'll just have to learn to be more careful. They will bite if you let them."

"Let me down!" Alyssaunde demanded, twisting herself around in the little man's grasp.

"Of course," the man agreed, setting her gently on the ground. "Ye'll not be trying to run away again, is it? Aha! And it isn't," he said, grabbing Alyssaunde again as she promptly tried to head off to the trees. "Now if ye want me to let ye loose, ye'll have to stay put."

"All right," Alyssaunde yelled, shaking herself free of his grasp. "But you'll suffer for this."

"My dear lady," the tall man said. "You must realize that we suffer already, or we would not be driven to such extreme measures. Now if you would please enter the flitterboat, we will be on our way."

Alyssaunde glared at him and stalked over to the flitter.

"Aha!" the little man said, leaping to follow her. "I'd best be along with ye as ye close the port, elsewise we might just be left outside."

Alyssaunde was rigid with suppressed rage. "That had occurred to me," she said.

"Now you wouldn't have left your friend behind," the tall man said.

"We both know that you wouldn't have dared harm him if I'd got safely away," Alyssaunde said.

"Good thinking," the tall man agreed. "In this case it's not true, but it *is* good thinking."

They went up the ramp, Alyssaunde first, O'Malley close behind, and the rest following. When they were in, the tall man pressed the plate that closed the port and retracted the ramp.

"You see," he said, "I've been in these flitter machines before. I know where things are."

"Then what do you want me for?" Alyssaunde asked icily.

"I don't know how to fly the craft," the tall man told her. "But you don't know what parts of it I don't know, so I wouldn't do anything overtly foolish if I were you."

"You can push me around," Alyssaunde said, "for the moment; you're bigger than I. But please don't give me advice."

The tall man thought this over while seating himself in one of the rear observer seats. "You're right," he said. "It is one thing to give you orders out of my own necessity, it is quite another to give you advice. I order you to get this thing in the air."

Alyssaunde settled carefully into the pilot's seat. O'Malley waved Carl into the seat beside her so that he and his companion could stay behind them. Carl reached over to take Alyssaunde's hand, to try to reassure her silently, and tell her that he would help if he could. Alyssaunde impatiently shook his hand off. With a twist of the control rods, she boosted the flitterboat high into the air.

"A good start," the tall man said. "Now if you would do me the favor of heading west, I would be in your debt."

"West," Alyssaunde said, flipping a few switches,

pushing a few buttons, and pulling back on a few control rods. The boat curved smoothly around and headed off in a new direction. The tall man checked the control panel and seemed satisfied. "Thank you," he said.

"You can't escape," Alyssaunde said. "I have no idea what you have in mind, but the Inspectors will pick you up wherever you go."

"They been trying these past two months," O'Malley said, "and they ain't got us yet."

"We have little option," the tall man said. "They chase us and we flee. Eventually either they will catch us or we will escape."

"Or you'll be killed," Alyssaunde said.

The tall man shrugged. "That is a form of escape," he said.

"Is there anything to eat aboard this craft?" the small man asked.

"No," Alyssaunde said.

The tall man reached behind him and palmed open a sliding door. The compartment revealed was filled with small aluminum trays with white plastic seals over the tops. He pulled one out and handed it to O'Malley. "Pull the tab," he said.

O'Malley pulled the tab on the side of the tray. It ran around three sides, and then the plastic top popped off. The tray was compartmented inside, and a different food was in each compartment: meat, a green vegetable of some leafy variety, rice, and what looked like a pudding. After it had been opened a few seconds a wisp of steam came up from the vegetable, then the whole tray was enveloped in a steam haze, which took about thirty seconds to clear away.

O'Malley poked cautiously at the meat. "Hot," he said. "I've never seen a thing like that before."

"It's an exothermic chemical reaction," the tall man said.

"Aye, but is it safe to eat?" O'Malley inquired.

TOMORROW KNIGHT 59

The tall man shrugged. "Safe enough," he said. "What are you worried about? The whole Inspector Force over the whole planet is after us, and you're worried about whether that's safe to eat?"

"I mistrust these artificial things," O'Malley said. "Food doesn't grow surrounded by tinfoil." He unsnapped the fork from the side of the tray and cautiously tasted the steaming food. He chewed it silently and speculatively for a minute before swallowing and taking the next bite. "Good," he finally pronounced.

"Good?" the tall man asked.

"Aye, for artificial food."

The tall man took another tray out, but then paused before unsnapping the tab. "I forget my manners," he said. "After all, I am host. Would either of you, ah, guests, like a tray?"

"Yes, thank you," Carl said. The tall man handed him one from the cabinet.

"Nice of you to offer me my own food," Alyssaunde said.

"Come on," the tall man said. "These flitters are all equipped with full supply cabinets before you take them out. The rental's the same by the day regardless of the supplies you use."

"You seem to know a fair amount about how the Guest Bureau works," Alyssaunde said.

"I do," the man agreed. "The unfortunate thing is that my training didn't go far enough. I learned how to service the things, but never how to fly them. It was discouraged, you understand. I'm sure you understand. You're a five, aren't you?"

"A five?" Carl asked.

"It's clear that you're not," the tall man said, "but the young lady—"

"I am," Alyssaunde agreed. "And I'll take a tray."

"What is a five?" Carl demanded.

"One of the ruling class," the tall man told him.

"One of the five in a thousand that has any say on what's going on in this segmented world of ours."

"I don't understand," Carl said.

The tall man handed Alyssaunde a tray. "Ask her to explain," he said.

Alyssaunde opened her tray and ate from it silently, watching the two men in the rear seats. "Who are you?" she asked finally. "What are you running from, and what do you want?"

The tall man nodded at his friend. "This is Mr. O'Malley," he said between forkfuls, "and I am Mr. Arthur."

"My moniker is Different O'Malley," the little man said. "And this here's Chester A. Arthur. We're pleased to make yer acquaintance. And who are yerselves?"

"Lance Corporal Carl Frederic Allan," Carl said.

"Alyssaunde," said Alyssaunde.

"A pleasure," Chester A. Arthur said. "There's no reason we can't be sociable during our brief sojourn together."

Alyssaunde put her tray down. "I admit that I've never been kidnapped at gunpoint before," she said, "so I may not be up on the proprieties, but I don't think it's required to be sociable with your kidnapper."

"I wish you wouldn't think of this as a kidnapping, Miz Alyssaunde," Chester A. Arthur said. "We are merely borrowing your piloting abilities for a while. We are not thieves or crooks, Miz Alyssaunde, we are renegades. We merely wish to escape the clutches of this society. If we could figure a way to leave this planet instead of merely fleeing to the Outlands, we would surely do that."

"You must have done something," Alyssaunde said, "committed some crime, or the Inspectors wouldn't be after you."

"That is a simplistic view of the universe," Chester

A. Arthur said. "Let me tell you about O'Malley and his crime. My friend here belongs to Sector Three, Area Five, which might not mean much to you, but he called it home. It was an analogue of Great Britain during the early Middle Ages, with a hereditary King John, and a hereditary Robin Hood, but mostly just simple artisans and craftsmen who sold their wares at the perennial village fairs that the Guests are so fond of attending."

Alyssaunde nodded at this. "I've been there," she said.

"So," Chester said.

Carl followed most of the description, except for the names. He just sat quietly and listened. Clearly there was a lot about his own world that he didn't know.

"O'Malley is a hunter," Chester continued. "An expert with the longbow, and no slouch with the hunting ax. His hunting party—four of you, was it?"

"Aye, four," O'Malley said.

"Four of them supplied meat to a few of the local villages. Then one day about a year ago they were out in the wood pursuing a great stag when a storm came up and they were forced to take shelter on some high ground. The storm lasted for about two days, completely washing out the trail they had been following. So they went around the long way, into an area of the wood unfamiliar to them.

"After a while they found a path, and they followed it. It led out of the wood and to a great paved road, the like of which they'd never seen. So they followed the road. Once and a while strange vehicles, like wagons with neither traces nor horses to pull them, came by on the road—"

"Great wains," O'Malley said. "They made a fearsome sound. Some could have carried a cottage inside."

"They didn't stop," Chester continued. "So the

party continued walking. After three or four hours walking they came to a great village, with stone houses many stories tall."

Alyssaunde nodded. "The next sector, Sector Two: Early Industrial New York. But that would mean—"

"Exactly," Chester agreed. "The barrier was down. The storm must have knocked it out. They never even knew when they crossed the line. As soon as they figured out what must have happened, they went to the nearest Inspector for assistance. They were all promptly arrested."

"Arrested?" Carl said. "But, what had they done?"

"You know you're not supposed to cross the barrier," Chester told him.

"But usually you *can't* cross the barrier," Carl said. "Certainly not on foot. It kind of shimmers in the air in front of you, and if you touch it you get a shock, and if you try to go through it, it kills you. But if the barrier was down, and they didn't even know where it was..."

"Ignorance," Chester said, "is no excuse under the law. Such law as there is. O'Malley and his companions were tried that afternoon and sentenced that evening. To the factories."

"The factories?" Carl asked.

"You have been kept in a state of ignorance, haven't you?" Chester said. "Where do you suppose they make all the good stuff that isn't made by hand, or by the 'cottage industries'?"

"What sort of stuff do you mean?" Carl asked.

"What about the armor you knights wear?"

"Some of it's handmade," Carl said.

"Out of what?"

"Sheets of iron and steel."

"From where?"

"They sell it at the PX."

"Invincible ignorance." Chester sighed. "Let's trace the chain down, Carl. Where does the PX get it?"

"I never thought about it," Carl said.

"And what about the armor that isn't handmade?"

"Some of it's issued, the rest is bought at the PX or one of the craft stores."

"OK, now: where does the PX get its supplies?"

"Like I said," Carl said, in an irritated voice, "I never thought about it. Are you telling me it's made at these factories?"

"That's right," Chester said. "And these flitterboats, and wristwatches, and all the other goodies except for a few that are imported from off planet, but you or I would never see those. All made at the factories by slave labor."

"Convict labor," Alyssaunde corrected.

"It's the same thing," Chester said, "when you can get convicted and sent up for walking through the wood after a rain."

Alyssaunde shook her head angrily. "The laws are made for everyone," she said, "and they have to be obeyed."

"Everyone?" Chester asked. "Even for you, Miz Alyssaunde?"

"That's not the same thing," Alyssaunde snapped, her face approaching red. "You know it isn't!"

"You can pass from sector to sector freely, from area to area with impunity. Daily you commit the same act for which my friend here was sentenced to a lifetime of drudgery and incarceration. For Mr. O'Malley it is a crime, for you it is an avocation. But then you fives make the laws, don't you?"

"It has to be done that way!" Alyssaunde insisted. "That's the way things work. If it wasn't done that way, then nobody would have anything."

"Who told you that?" Chester asked. "You learn it in school?"

"You can't just have the people from one sector going over to another sector whenever they feel like it," Alyssaunde insisted. "All the cultures are so different that there'd be no degree of realism at all unless they're kept separate."

"And what's it all for, Miz Alyssaunde, what's it all for?" Chester asked, smiling grimly at her.

"For the Guests, of course. You know that."

"Did you?" Chester asked Carl. "Did you know that Earth is all just one big tourist show? That all of the sectors are recreations from Earth's past? Amusements for the aliens?"

"Not exactly," Carl said. "I never really thought about it. You know, sometimes I did wonder just what we were fighting about."

"It was all just a big show—meaningless. What do you think of that?"

Carl shrugged. "It's one way to make a living," he said. "No worse than most."

"You don't feel used, exploited?" Chester asked.

"Not really," Carl said. "I do think they could let us travel around. But then, when I become a knight I'll be able to visit the other sectors. I think that's true—at least, that's what they say."

"Aye," O'Malley said. "The other sectors in yer own area." He chucked his food tray into the waste receptacle Chester pointed out to him and glumly watched it disappear down the chute. "When ye've made knight ye're really somebody. They'll actually allow ye to transfer to sectors where they have more need of ye."

"This is all very fascinating," Alyssaunde said. "But I'd just as soon not continue it any longer than necessary. If you gentlemen would tell me where you'd like to be dropped, I shall see about the dropping."

Chester studied the control board. The locator said 03:02:C/5. "We're heading the right way," he said. "There's a large Outland on the other side of Area Five. You can let us off anywhere in there."

"But that must be twelve hundred miles," Alyssaunde said. "It'll take six hours to get there."

"I guess we'll be real friendly at the end of six hours," Chester said, leaning back. Alyssaunde glared at him, but couldn't think of anything to say.

The silence stretched on. Carl, still weak from his wounds, closed his eyes and quickly fell asleep. When he woke up, about half an hour later, nothing had changed except that O'Malley was now also stretched out and his eyes closed. Slight snorting noises escaped from his mouth with every breath. Chester A. Arthur was leaning back, completely relaxed, but his eyes were open and watchful. Alyssaunde was staring out the viewport.

Carl looked out the port by his seat. It was pitch dark outside, and he couldn't see a thing. "What are you looking at?" he asked Alyssaunde.

"My life is passing by underneath the flitter," she said. "Do you know what I mean?"

"I don't think so," Carl said cautiously.

Alyssaunde turned to him and took his hand. "I've been taught certain things all my life," she said. "Just as you have. I'm just as much a prisoner of my training and my environment as you are of yours."

"I never thought that I was," Carl said.

Alyssaunde took his hand. "Neither did I," she said.

"Very touching," came the harsh voice of Chester A. Arthur from the back of the cabin.

Carl turned to him. "You never told us," he said. "What happened to make you a renegade? What are you running away from?"

"The same factory that O'Malley graced," Chester said, "there graced I, also."

"You escaped together?" Alyssaunde asked.

"That's right."

"How did you get there? What did you do?"

"You know," Chester said, "all my life I used to hear that that was the one question you never asked a prisoner: What did you do? That the information was his to give or keep, and that it was a deadly insult to violate this rule."

"Oh," Alyssaunde said. "I didn't know, I'm sorry."

"No, that's not it. The point is that when I got sent up I learned that the first thing any two prisoners talk about when they get together is what each of them did. A guy will walk over to you and say: 'Hi, my name is John Johnson, and I robbed a blind man in a candy store; what did you do?' Just the most casual thing in the world."

"They brag about it?" Alyssaunde asked.

"No, it's not bragging, it's more like an identity tag. What you're in for is just as important as your name, you see. Very curious, if you think about it."

"So," Carl said, "what were you in for? And how did you escape?"

Chester considered, staring off into the roof of the flitter.

"If you don't want to tell, it's OK," Alyssaunde said.

"No, it's not that," Chester said. "I'm just trying to decide what to say; picking my words, as it were."

"Oh."

"I was born and brought up in Sanloo," Chester said.

"The city!" Carl said. "I've heard of it, but I've never met anyone from Sanloo before."

"You've never met anyone from anywhere before," Chester said. "No insult intended, but you've led a very sheltered life."

"I was in my first battle at the age of fourteen," Carl said. "You call that sheltered?"

"Yes," Chester said. "And I have a feeling that by the time this night is out, so will you. At any rate, we were a Plebe family, but I was a very bright child, so I quickly rose to the top of the plebe heap. A short climb, but once there I could go no higher."

"Plebe?" Carl asked.

"Skill in battle," Chester told him, "is not necessarily a sign of sophistication. It is fair to call you sheltered. Miz Alyssaunde here has never, I warrant, fought a battle in her life, at least not with a sword, and she is far less sheltered than you."

"But far more sheltered than I had thought, apparently," Alyssaunde said.

"A plebe," Chester told Carl, "is a member of the serving class. Born in the know but not in the nobility. Born to serve the fives and the Guests. Plebes are servants in the fives' houses, and staff the hotels, and service the machines, and keep everything running. The Inspectors are high-class plebes."

"What do the fives do?" Carl asked.

"They are the administrators," Alyssaunde said, somewhat more sharply than she intended. "They make all the decisions. They shoulder the responsibilities. Without them to supply the grease and the direction, the whole machine would fall apart in a month!"

"That's one way to look at it," Chester said.

"How do you look at it?" Carl asked.

"I don't want to hear," Alyssaunde said.

"Cover your ears," Chester instructed her. He turned to Carl. "They give the orders. They sign the papers. They make the money."

"That's not fair!" Alyssaunde insisted. "Someone has to give the orders."

O'Malley opened his right eye and raised his right hand. "I volunteer," he said. Then he closed his eye and began snoring softly again.

"At any rate," Chester said, "putting aside this philosophical discussion for now, I became a historian, a very important job on this planet. For a five, you understand, it would be a profession, but for me it was merely a job. I worked for a five named Cappa Neb-Ogallala. He was a chief historian. That meant that I did all the work, while he signed his name to all the documents we produced. I did all the research in the back stacks of the Earth Artifacts Library and the Government House Library, but whenever I wanted a book, he had to sign it out."

"And this embittered you," Alyssaunde said, "you doing all the work, and Neb-Ogallala getting all the credit?"

"No," Chester told her. "It's funny, but it didn't. It does now, when I look back on it, but at the time I thought I was one of the luckiest men on Earth to have my job. I really enjoyed it, you see. And as for Neb-Ogallala signing all the papers, well, I just thought that's the way things were."

"You read books all day," Carl said wonderingly, "and this was your job? And sometimes you wrote things, and they paid you for that?"

"It's better than beating at strangers with swords," Chester A. Arthur said.

Carl sniffed. "Is not," he said. "An ancient and honorable profession, soldiering."

Chester thought it over. "That's true," he said. "And it's certainly not your fault that your soldiering is done in a less than noble cause."

"What is the function of all this history studying?" Carl asked.

"We keep the sectors on line," Chester told him. "Whenever there is a question from one of the sectors about whether something is an anachronism or not, we research it and file a report. On the basis of our research, the Council decides whether to allow whatever it is."

"It must have been fascinating work," Alyssaunde said.

Chester smiled at her. "The best sort of thing a plebe could ever hope to do."

"Listen," Alyssaunde said, "you overdo this inequality bit, you know. The work you did would absolutely fascinate me; I've spent a good bit of time reading about the history of Earth and studying what texts were available. But I could never get the job, or the five analogue of it, because I'm a woman. A five perhaps, but still a woman, and unsuited for any sort of work involving anything more complex than breaking an egg into a dish."

"No doubt," Chester said, nodding his head. "I never claimed to have an exclusive franchise on prejudice. Everyone suffers from it to some extent or another. We are all bound by the artificial fetters of our culture and our laws. Some of us merely have silken cords instead of rough hemp ropes."

"How did you end up in the factory?" Carl asked.

"I made a discovery," Chester said. "At first I was doubtful, and thought I must be mistaken. But the more I researched, the more all sorts of threads came into place and made it clear that I was right. An exceptionally startling discovery that would upset much that we believe. I told this discovery to Neb-Ogallala. He demanded proof. I gave him proof. He forbade me from ever mentioning it to anyone again. I insisted that it be brought before the Council. I was arrested within the week."

"What did you discover?" Carl asked.

"I don't think I should tell you now," Chester said. "It would serve no purpose, and would cause you nothing but trouble whether you believed me or not. Someday, perhaps, I will see that the word gets out, but not now."

"What did they charge you with?" Alyssaunde asked.

"Charge?" Chester said. "Why, they never did charge me with anything. They just locked me away in a holding cell for a few weeks, then transferred me to a factory. I was warned not to continue making seditious remarks, or I couldn't stay at the factory. I asked the guard what seditious remarks I had made, and where they could send me that was worse than the factory, and he told me that he was merely obeying orders and I'd better just shut up. I asked him to show me my conviction papers, and he told me they knew what to do with troublemakers of my sort. So I shut up."

"How did you escape?" Alyssaunde asked.

Chester looked at her. "I don't think I'd better tell you," he said. "I may have to do it again." He got up and reached over Alyssaunde's head. "I'm going to wake O'Malley up now," he said, "and get some sleep myself. Since Different doesn't know these flitters at all, I'm going to disconnect the communicator first. Just so you don't suffer from temptation."

He opened a panel over the pilot's seat, removed a slim circuit board, and stuck it in his pocket. Then he shook O'Malley awake.

"Huh?" O'Malley sat up and balled his hands into fists. "Where are ye? What ye want? Stand still!" He yelled, twisting around in his seat. "Oh, it's ye, Chester." He relaxed. "My watch, is it?"

"Right," Chester said. "Wake me after two hours. We should not land, or even turn, during that time. If anything changes that you don't understand, no mater how trivial, wake me immediately."

"I surely shall," O'Malley agreed.

Chester settled back in his chair to sleep, and Carl did likewise. This time he went into a deep, dreamless sleep and did not wake for some time.

❀ 7 ❀

When Carl awoke dawn was just starting to light up the landscape behind them. He looked over at the control board just in time to see the locator change from 05:01:A/8, to -0:-U:-/T. The other three were awake and silently watching the mountainous scenery passing below.

"We're there," Alyssaunde said. She stretched and then took the controls, moving the flitter closer to the ground.

"Not yet," Chester told her. "A little bit farther and we'll be through the mountains, if the map was right. Say about another ten minutes. Then just find a clear spot and let us out. After which you can go about your business, and we'll go about ours, and sorry to have inconvenienced you."

Alyssaunde shook her head. "You can't accomplish anything, you know."

"There's a couple of thousand square miles of Outland here to disappear in," Chester said. "That will buy us enough time to figure out what we want to accomplish; which, after all, is the first job."

In about six minutes the mountains dropped away to foothills, and then flattened to a beautiful green valley. Alyssaunde guided the flitterboat down to a wide grassland next to a lake and landed. "You realize that I'll have to report all this immediately," she said.

"I'm keeping the piece I removed from your communicator," Chester told her. "The time it takes you to get somewhere and report this will be enough for us to have thoroughly disappeared when they send out a search party. I thank you, Miz Alyssaunde, for your kindness."

"Let's take some of them food trays," O'Malley said.

"A brilliant notion," Chester agreed. They found a canvas bag in the supply locker, and loaded up the food trays.

Chester palmed the door switch, and the hatch opened and the ramp dropped. "Good-bye, Corporal Allan," Chester said. "Think over what we've discussed. I hope we meet again someday. And you too, Miz Alyssaunde. I hope you don't regard this as an altogether unfortunate experience."

"Well," she said, "it has been an experience, I'll grant you that."

Chester A. Arthur and Different O'Malley walked down the ramp and onto the grass, still wet with the morning dew. They had taken no more than ten steps when five black Inspectors' flitterboats dropped out of the sky, surrounding them.

"Drop your weapons," an amplified voice boomed from one of the black flitters, "and don't move! You haven't a chance."

Chester and Different looked at each other. O'Malley shrugged. They both dropped their guns and the sack of food trays and raised their hands.

Black uniformed Inspectors dropped out of the black flitterboats and closed in on the two men. A couple of the Inspectors dogtrotted over to the flitter Carl and Alyssaunde were in and came up the ramp. "Another one!" one of them said, grabbing Carl.

"Are you all right, Miz Alyssaunde?" the other asked.

"Fine," Alyssaunde said. "How did you people get here?"

"Your father got worried when you didn't come

home to dinner last night," he told her. "Finally he tried calling your flitter, but your communicator was out. So he told us, and we put a trace on your command frequency. We've been following you on screens all across the country. When you got close to the Outlands, we put these flitters in the air a couple of minutes behind you. We had reason to believe those two men were in the area you left from, so it seemed a reasonable precaution. Who's this third one?" he indicated Carl.

"He's a soldier from that sector," Alyssaunde said. "His name is Corporal Allan. He's been wounded."

"We'll take care of him, miz," the Inspector said. And the two of them helped Carl down the ramp. The last glimpse he had of Alyssaunde was her face staring after him as the Inspectors took him across to one of their ships.

Carl spent the next three weeks in a hospital. It wasn't until the third week that he figured out that he was a prisoner. "I want to go back to my bivouac," he told the doctor treating him.

"That's up to the Inspectors," the doctor told him. "You're in the detainment wing."

"But what have I done?" he demanded.

"I'm your doctor, not your judge," the doctor said. "But you must have done something. The Inspectors are anxious to take you away."

It was during the third week that he got mail: a letter from His Majesty Hiram VI himself. When he saw the envelope he was as elated as the third hour of a happy drunk. The letter itself sobered him up quickly:

HIRAM VI
KING OF THE CELTS & PICTS & JUTES
EMPEROR OF ROME-IN-EXILE
Hereditary Foe of the Supremacy of Allah
PRIME AREA, SECTOR 7

14 May 697
TO: Former Lance Corporal Carl Frederic Allan
Greetings.
We were sorry to hear of the wounds suffered in our defense.
We cannot, of course, condone your subsequent action.
In view of your record up to that time, and your heroism in your last action, your father's pension will not be cut.
We hope this reassures you.
Your Imperial Majesty,

Hiram VI

There was a pen-scratched *H* in the signature block. His king had disowned him. But at least his father's pension wouldn't suffer. Carl didn't find this reassuring, since it had never occurred to him that his father's pension *might* suffer. Now he had to worry about all the other things they might do to him that he hadn't considered before. Once he put his mind to it he could think of a lot. He was afraid to ask about any of them, because he might just put the idea into their heads.

The Inspectors were waiting for him to be well enough to take away. One of them, a tall, dour-looking man who didn't speak, came in to check him over every couple of days. It was only Carl's physical condition that interested him. He had no questions to ask Carl, and wasn't interested in any answers.

"If he won't talk to me," Carl complained to the doctor one evening after the Inspector's visit, "what does he keep coming for? Can't he just get your reports?"

"He doesn't want to have to tell anyone that he relied on the doctor's word for the patient's condition," the doctor explained. "They're conditioned not to believe anyone, or at least not to accept anyone's word without checking."

When the doctor and the Inspector agreed that Carl was well enough, he was taken before a board of three judges. "Of what am I accused?" he asked them.

"Silence!" the one on Carl's right ordered.

"You have already been tried and found guilty," the middle one told him. "This is the sentencing hearing."

"I was tried and found guilty without even being present?" Carl asked, amazed. They didn't do things that way in his sector.

"You are convicted of the crime of being found out of your sector," the middle judge explained, looking bored. "Two Inspectors swore to it. Can you refute their testimony?"

"No," Carl said, "but the circumstances—"

"The circumstances are none of our concern!" the left judge said sharply. "What is now of our concern is what to do with this man."

"He may be contaminated," the right judge said.

"He may," the middle judge agreed. "Then we must put him with the others."

"The island?" the left judge asked.

"The island!" the right judge stated.

"The island!" the middle judge agreed. He rapped his gavel. "Carl Frederic Allan, you are sentenced to an indefinite term of service on Devil's Island; term to commence immediately."

And the Inspectors took Carl away and they put him in a little cell. During the course of the day several more men were put into the cell or the one adjoining it. At the end of the day they were each given a tin bowl of soup and a hunk of bread to sop it up with. Then they were lined up, and chained together with leg irons, and led out single-file to a covered van.

The van took them to a large flying craft that looked like an oversized, bulbous flitter, and they were herded aboard.

The flier took them all to Devil's Island.

❈ 8 ❈

They flew over water for a long time before reaching Devil's Island. Carl asked a guard what sea it was, and got a silent glare as his answer. The island was fairly large, as such things go, maybe twelve or fourteen miles in diameter on the average.

Carl spent the first two days in a holding area, and then was assigned to his barracks and his task. The barracks were primitive, long, one-story wooden buildings housing about forty men each, lined up in neat rows in a muddy field. Carl was put in the building crew, constructing more barracks.

At the end of the first week Carl spotted Chester A. Arthur in the mess hall and went over to sit with him. The restrictions were very loose on the island; the guards weren't worried about escapes. There was no place to go. Sometimes a fed-up resident—they weren't called prisoners for some reason lost in the bureaucracy of the system—ran off into the surrounding jungle. Within a few days he crept back to camp. Or else he never came back. As long as he didn't leave the island, it was all the same to the guards.

"I'm sorry to see you here," Chester said. "I knew they'd kept you, but I thought you'd get some easier factory. You've never tried to escape or otherwise caused them rouble."

"They're afraid I'm contaminated," Carl said.

Chester laughed. "With what?" he asked.

"With you, I think," Carl said.

That sobered Chester up. He thought about it for a few long minutes, chewing on the vegetable stew that was their evening meal. "You must be right," he finally decided. "Maybe your friend Alyssaunde will be able to do something for you."

"She never even came to see me," Carl said. "She's not my friend."

"Clearly," Chester agreed. He sighed. "Well, since we got you into this ... Do you want to leave?"

"Leave?"

"Escape."

"Yes," Carl said. "Only—how, and where to?"

Chester shrugged. "What difference does it make?" he asked. "The worst they can do to you is send you back here."

"They can kill you," Carl said.

"True," Chester agreed. "But I still say the worst they can do to you is send you back here."

"It's not so bad," Carl said.

"It grows on you," Chester told him. "Wait till you've been here a while. It's the awful monotony more than anything else. It's not that the food is bad so much, although it is, it's that it's always the same."

Carl pushed at his stew. "Well, I don't want to spend the rest of my life here, which is what they seem to have in mind. And they taught us in the army that the best time to effect an escape is as soon as possible, before you get used to being a prisoner. What do we do?"

"We build a giant dugout canoe," Chester said.

Carl stared at him. "Where?" he asked. "In front of the barracks?"

"About a half mile up the coast," Chester said. "We take turns, whenever we can get away. The most important thing is stealing food."

"This food?" Carl said. "For what?"

"For O'Malley. He ran away the day after we got here, and he's been there ever since."

"You're serious about this, then."

"Of course," Chester said. "What did you think?"

"Well, what do we do with this canoe? Which way do we paddle?"

"I think we can manage a sail," Chester said.

"All right then, sail. Which way?"

"That, I admit, is a problem," Chester said. "We have no idea where we are. They change directions several times, with no consistent pattern, when they fly us in here. And there are no windows in the prisoners' compartment."

"So?" Carl said.

"We're working on it."

"Listen," Carl said. "Much as I'd like to leave here and get myself killed by the Inspectors, I'm not going anywhere until you pick a direction."

"I told you we're working on it," Chester said, sounding annoyed. "I have several methods in mind, but they are all useless until we have the means of escape at hand. My feeling is that the island isn't too far from land, and the length of the trip is just to confuse the prisoners. Most islands are on the continental shelves, close to their continent."

"I thought there were islands in the middle of the oceans."

"Sometimes," Chester said. "But they're almost always volcanic. There's no volcano anywhere on this island."

Convinced by this logic, Carl went to sleep with happy thoughts of escape that night, but woke up in the middle of the night dreaming that a volcano had just thrust itself up under his straw cot. He didn't sleep well for the rest of the night.

The next day it rained. While the rest of the residents went up to the great windowless stone slab up on the hill that was the local factory, Carl and the others in the building crew were off work. Ancient established custom has it that you can't build houses in the rain, it's bad luck. Carl took a spare two-by-four and a bowl of cold vegetable stew and slogged through the rain the quarter-mile to O'Malley and the felled tree that was going to become a canoe.

"It's good to see ye, lad," O'Malley told him "Although I'm sure ye don't feel the same. But take heart, we'll all be away from here in no time."

"How long do you think it's going to take to turn that log into a canoe?" Carl asked.

"I don't know," O'Malley said. "It took a week just to cut it down. But it should go faster from now on."

"Wonderful," Carl said. "Well, just tell me what tools you need, and I'll try to obtain them for you from the work crew." They crouched together under the newly hewn log to keep out of the rain. It wasn't really wide enough to keep them dry, but it provided some psychological comfort. "How do you like being out here all alone most of the time?" Carl asked.

O'Malley raised his head and spat out into the rain. "Not so bad," he said. "Most of the time it's not so bad. I'm beginning to think I'm going slightly crazy, hearing things late at night, but I've decided not to worry about it. Once we leave this island paradise, I'm sure it will stop."

"What sort of things?" Carl asked.

"Rumblings deep in the earth," Different O'Malley told him. "Strange and curious noises that get louder and louder and then fade away again and disappear. They seem to come at a regular time each night."

"Rumblings?" Carl said, trying to remember what he knew about volcanoes.

"That's what I said," O'Malley said, glaring at him. "Ye're not going to laugh at me now, are ye? Make me sorry I told ye?"

"Not a bit," Carl said. "I don't think it's at all funny. You haven't noticed it getting hot, have you?"

"Every day," O'Malley said, giving him a strange look.

"No, I mean the ground. You haven't noticed the ground getting warm, have you, when you hear the rumbling?"

"No," O'Malley said. "It just rumbles for a while, then stops. About an hour after sunset most nights. Regular as dripping water."

"Have you told Arthur?" Carl asked.

"Told me what?" Chester A. Arthur demanded, stepping out from behind a tree. "And please call me 'Chester,' and not 'Arthur,' if you don't mind. Mr. Arthur is all right, I suppose. You have no idea how confusing it can be to have two first names."

"About the rumbling," Carl said.

"Rumbling?" Chester crouched down and tried to fit himself under the downed log with his two companions. He was only moderately successful.

"I been hearing noises, Chester," O'Malley said, looking sheepish. "I been alone so much, I suppose."

"Rumbling?" Chester asked.

"Aye, rumblings. About an hour after sundown. Deep in the earth, I would say."

"Rumbling!" Chester said, staring at the raindrops hitting the water.

"I'm sure it will stop when we get away from here," O'Malley said.

"Rumbling!" Chester said again, staring now at the ground beneath his feet. "An hour after sundown, you say. At no other time?"

"Aye, at other times, too. The noise has awakened me during the night occasionally, and sometimes I think I've heard it during the day."

"Earthquake, do you think?" Carl asked. "Perhaps that volcano coming up out of the ground."

"I don't remember too much about earthquakes," Chester said, "but I don't believe they're so selective. If Different could hear it here, then we could surely hear it half a mile away at camp. Same with an uprushing volcano. It seems to have stopped raining," he added, sticking his hand out. He stepped out from under the log, stood up to his full six foot eight, and stretched. "But it hasn't stopped dripping," he added, as the tree he was under gave up a part of its acquired water, cascading it onto his bare head.

"Then ye think it's in my mind?" O'Malley asked.

"I didn't say so, and I don't think so," Chester said. "Let me consider it for a while. As a matter of fact, let me stay here this evening and see if I can hear it."

Carl and O'Malley joined Chester, who had walked to a nearby rock and was standing glaring out over the sea. The water was choppy and the waves coming in fast, beaten up by a stiff wind. But the same wind was blowing the storm clouds rapidly down the coast, clearing the sky behind them, and a full rainbow arced across the eastern sky.

A gaily colored flitterboat appeared high in the sky, coming straight in toward them. Carl pointed it out to his two companions. "Look," he said, "you don't see many of those around here."

"I've not seen one before since coming to this island," O'Malley said. "I suppose there's nothing worth staring at here."

"I imagine this island isn't on any of their maps or lists of happenings," Chester said.

As they watched, three black Inspectors' flitterboats came out of the clouds to the west and intercepted the Guest flitter. They closed in on it, surrounding it, and must have communicated with the Guest inside, for presently all four flitterboats flew off together to the west.

"We're in quarantine," Chester said. "Unapproachable. Which explains why we haven't seen any Guests about. The sight of our fetters might depress them."

"What fetters?" Carl asked.

"I speak metaphorically," Chester told him.

"Some of us," O'Malley commented, "have been known to attempt to make off with yon Guests' flitterboats in an unlawful and unfriendly manner. I name no names, ye understand. But I've heard it's so."

"No!" Chester said. "Why anybody who would do a thing like that would be a criminal. I can't believe it."

O'Malley nodded his head sagely. " 'Tis true," he said, " 'Tis a pity, but 'tis true."

"Well, we've learned one thing," Carl said, staring after the retreating craft.

"What's that?" Chester asked curiously.

"Why, the direction of the closest land," Carl told him. He pointed. "That's where the Inspectors came from, and it's where they're going back to."

Chester slapped him on the back. "Boy," he said, "glad to have you along. I should have picked up on that myself. Very good."

"Then it helps?" Carl asked.

"Any truth," Chester said, "no matter how obscure, or seemingly unimportant, is a piece of the mosaic and a step toward completion. That's what it says over the door of the Earth Artifacts Library."

"But what about the direction?"

"You're right, the flitterboats point the way to the closest shore. But the rumbling points the way of our escape."

Carl sat down on the rock. "The rumble," he said.

"Did you ever wonder where the guards go when they're off?" Chester asked.

"Let's stick with the rumble for a while," Carl said. "Explain that to me first."

"I am," Chester said. "There are three shifts of guards, right?"

"Right," Carl agreed. "So?"

"So they all spend their off-duty time in the guard building, right? I mean, you never see one outside anywhere except when they're on duty."

"I guess so," Carl said. "I haven't thought about it."

"And, come to think of it, no flitterboat ever comes to take the off-duty guards for leaves or passes."

"That's true," Carl said. "I've never seen a guard either come to or leave the island."

"And the guardhouse is not that large," Chester said.

"What does that mean?" Carl asked.

"It means I know where we are, and how to get away from here." Chester A. Arthur squatted on the rock and turned from Carl to O'Malley, staring them both intently in the face. "And I know what we should do when we get away from here. That's what I came along to tell you. There's only one logical thing. It's been staring me in the face, but I've been unwilling to see it."

"I don't think I'm overly fond of yer imagery," O'Malley said. "What should we do?"

"How are we getting away from there?" Carl asked.

"The rumbling noise," Chester said. "It's not your overworked imagination, O'Malley, it's a subway."

"A which?" O'Malley asked.

"A sort of a train that goes through a hole in the ground."

"What's it doing down there?" O'Malley asked.

Chester shrugged. "Nobody knows," he said. "It's incredibly ancient. Been here longer than we have. It's from the elder civilization."

"What does that mean?" Carl asked.

Chester put his arm on Carl's shoulder. "Are you ready for that great truth I warned you about?"

Carl nodded. "I suppose so," he said. "If my knowing it is what got me here, then I should really know it, shouldn't I?"

Chester nodded. "Then here it is: This is not the Earth."

There was a prolonged silence while both Carl and

O'Malley stared at him. The waves hitting the beach made the only sound.

"This," Carl repeated, "is not the Earth?"

"Ye're not having us on?" O'Malley demanded.

"That's what I found out," Chester said, "and that's why I'm here."

"Then where are we," Carl asked, "and where is Earth?"

"How do you know?" O'Malley asked.

"My historical research," Chester said. "Earth has only one moon. A few other little things like that. So I started to dig. I found the maps of this planet and compared them with the historical maps of Earth. They're different."

"Well," Carl said, "it's been a long time. Things change over a long time."

"The shape and number of the continents don't change in the few thousand years you're calling a long time," Chester told him. "This, I repeat, *is not Earth*. These trees are not Earth trees, this ocean is not an ocean of Earth, this atmosphere is not Earth's air. We have been lied to all our lives about the basic fact of our existence. Something even more basic and important than the phony war games you were playing. Our ancestors are not buried in the soil of this planet. The pyramids, weather-beaten with age, are, at most, a couple of hundred years old. Probably not that."

"Ye said ye had a plan, and knew what we should do," O'Malley said. "What is it we should do?"

"Escape," Chester said.

O'Malley sighed. "Isn't that what we've been trying to do these past weeks? Is that not what I've been doing out here in the rain?"

"I didn't mean from the island," Chester said, "but from the planet. We leave here and make our way to Sanloo and the spaceport. Once there, we must board a ship and leave this planet, whatever its name is, and find our way to Earth—the real Earth."

"And then what?" O'Malley asked.

"And then find a way to stop this farce, to let the people of this planet live useful lives that are not playacting. And without Guests looking over their shoulders with every act."

Carl thought back over his past, remembering the times he had been fighting for his life with two or three flitters hovering over him and various nonhuman heads peering down through the viewports. "I'm for that," he said.

"What can the three of us possibly do against this whole planet, do ye suppose?" O'Malley asked.

"It won't be against the whole planet," Chester said. "Just the fives."

"Well, then," O'Malley amended, "what can we three do against all the fives?"

"I don't know," Chester said. "We'll have to find out."

O'Malley shrugged. "Why not?" he said.

The three of them stayed there talking until the sun went down. Then Carl stretched out on a clear plot of grass near the downed log and stared up at the heavens, leaving the other two to stay up on their rock and debate. *These are the wrong stars,* he found himself thinking. *These are not the stars my ancestors saw.* He felt immeasurably cheated by not having been told in his youth. The fact that the wars he'd been fighting since he was fourteen were only games didn't bother him much; he had never really thought of them as anything else. The higher strategies were out of his sphere anyway. But the stars ...

"You know," Carl said to nobody in particular, "when I was a kid I used to spend nights lying on the grass and staring at the stars and thinking about all the ages of people before me who had stared at the same stars. Only they didn't."

"I know what you mean, Carl," Chester said. "I used to wander about to the different mounds and wonder what fabled cities lay buried under them, and what mythical people had walked the streets. New York, perhaps, or Rome, or Carthage. Only they weren't."

"What are the mounds, then?" Carl asked.

Chester shrugged. "Traces of the elder race," he replied. "Just like the subway."

"What elder race?"

"Some people that lived here before we Earthmen arrived, and disappeared before we got to meet any of them. We have found pictures of them, and they don't correspond to any of the intelligent races we know about. Which doesn't mean anything, of course; the universe is too large for our knowledge to be anything but fragmentary."

"And the cities they built are now mounds, but yet their subways still work?"

"Apparently the cities are from their prehistory," Chester said, "while the subways are from right before they left."

Somehing strange impinged upon Carl's consciousness. It took him a few seconds to figure out what it was, then he realized that the ground beneath him was beginning to rumble.

"It's happening," O'Malley said. "Feel it?"

"Indeed," Chester said.

"Why is it that we can hear it here," Carl asked, "and not in camp?"

Chester shook his head. "Not sure," he said. "Perhaps it's closer to the surface here, perhaps it's merely a different rock formation."

"Well," O'Malley said, patting his downed log fondly. "There's little point in staying around here any longer. Let's get back to camp, where the transportation is."

9

O'Malley slept in a bed that night for the first time in a month. The unaccustomed softness kept him awake, and he stayed up most of the night smiling softly into the darkness. When Carl woke up O'Malley was finally asleep, but he was still smiling.

Chester A. Arthur came into the barracks while Carl was standing in line, patiently waiting his turn at the basin. "Put your coveralls on," Chester said. "I've got to show you something. Where's O'Malley?"

"Still asleep," Carl said.

"Wake him," Chester said, "and meet me outside."

So Carl woke O'Malley and ducked, as O'Malley reacted with a clenched fist to being pulled from his dream.

"Oh, it's ye, lad," O'Malley said, sitting up and scratching his hair. "What's happening?"

"Chester wants us outside," Carl said. "I don't know why. It's ten minutes to breakfast."

"Breakfast?" O'Malley asked, rubbing his hands together. "Now, I could use some breakfast, indeed I could. What sort of provender does this miserable island supply?"

"There are two basic breakfasts for the prisoners," Carl said. "The first is thick corn gruel, and the second is thin corn gruel. The second is more common than the first."

"Ye know how to excite a man's appetite," O'Malley told him, pulling his coveralls on. "Give me a second at the tile wall and I'll be with ye."

When they got outside Chester led them around two buildings and to the side of the guardhouse. "Look," he said.

In the clearing in front of the guardhouse a line of prisoners were having leg shackles put on by a very bored pair of blacksmiths.

"For this," O'Malley said, "ye're having us miss our gruel? I've seen it before."

"Have you?" Chester asked. "Then don't you notice anything odd about it?"

O'Malley stared. "Nope," he said finally. "That's the way we did it in our little squirage jail in my sector."

"But that wasn't how they did it when they brought us here," Chester said. "Remember?"

"Sure it is," O'Malley said. "They cuffed our legs."

"Like that?"

O'Malley stared again. "No," he said. "Come to think of it, not like that at all. They had shiny cuffs that opened with a tiny key. Very fancy."

"And a lot easier to open and close than those great iron rings," Chester said.

"That's true," O'Malley admitted. "Then why do ye suppose they're going back to the old way?"

"See those three gentlemen sitting across the field?" Chester asked.

"Aye. Ye mean the ones in the fancy uniforms. What of them?"

"What do you think of them, Carl?"

Carl squinted across the field at the three men, who were sitting around a low wooden table sipping from glass mugs. "Two uniforms, I would say," Carl said. "An officer and a sergeant. The third is civilian dress of some sort, although I've never seen the like before."

"If I've got it figured out properly," Chester said, "they're our tickets out of here."

"I'm all agog," O'Malley said without enthusiasm. "Explain yourself."

"The second day we were here," Chester said, "I noticed another pickup like this. As soon as the preparations are complete, those prisoners are going to be led into the guardhouse. And, as I should have realized earlier, they are not going to come out again."

"Yer subway," O'Malley said.

"Right. They're going off to work in some sector, and the men in the gray uniforms are their escorts."

O'Malley nodded his head sadly. "I should have guessed," he said. "And ye're going to suggest any second that we march out there and get ourselves shackled to the rest of them."

"Not a bit of it," Chester said.

"That's a relief," Carl said, trying to fight down the feeling of imminent doom that was building inside of him.

"We're going to dispose of those gentlemen in the gray suits," Chester said, "and take their places."

"You're crazy," Carl said, as the feeling of doom settled in his stomach. "We could never get near them. And what good will it do?"

"The problem," Chester explained, "has been finding a way to get into the underground railway. We certainly can't go in as prisoners. Not that the place is particularly well guarded; they rely mostly on secrecy. What prisoner would want to break into the guardhouse? But there are certain to be enough guards just casually hanging around to overpower the three of us, or at least give the alarm.

"I first thought of us going in as guards, since the different shifts don't seem to know each other very well, but that presented some insurmountable problems. It might work for one man with a lot of nerve and commensurate luck, but never for three. Then, this morning, I woke up to a lot of yelling going on outside my barracks. These poor unfortunates were being rounded up and marched to the guardhouse to be shackled. I remembered the last time, and the men in gray. And it came to me."

Carl had control of his stomach again. "Let's hear it," he said.

"Those men," Chester said, nodding his chin toward the uniformed visitors across the field, "don't know the guards, and the guards don't know them. And the new shift of guards comes on duty in about ten minutes, so the ones they pass going out won't even be the same ones they passed coming in."

"Those men," O'Malley said, "are about fifteen feet from the nearest building, clear out in the open. How do ye expect to—ah—get their attention?"

"Ah," Chester said. "For that we need the aid of a guard."

Carl shook his head. "Which guard," he asked, "would you like me to ask?"

"All you want to do is borrow his costume for a few minutes," Chester said. "O'Malley will help you persuade one."

And so ten minutes later Carl, newly shaved and with his moustache trimmed for maximum effect, donned a guard's uniform. The guard, trussed up and gagged, glared at him and mouthed inarticulate curses through the gag.

"Keep a civil tongue in yer head," O'Malley snapped, kicking the guard in the foot.

"What do you care what he's saying," Carl said. "You can't understand him with that gag in his mouth."

"No, but I can imagine what I'd be saying in his position, and I don't want to hear it," O'Malley said. "I think I'll take him out of here and put him under cover for a while." O'Malley tossed the guard over his shoulder like a sack of millet and stalked out of the barracks room with him.

Carl strode back and forth between the rows of cots in the empty barracks, practicing walking like a guard. There was a certain strut in the stride of the camp guards that was not in the walk of the prisoners, and if Carl didn't have it another guard would immediately spot him as a phony, probably without even knowing why.

When he felt he had the walk down, Carl headed back to where Chester A. Arthur was waiting. He walked conscientiously down the middle of the street, looking neither to the right nor the left, despite a strong urge to dash into the nearest doorway every time anyone—prisoner or guard—came in sight.

When Carl came up to the building behind which Chester was waiting, Chester clapped his hands softly together in appreciation. "Very good," he said. "As you walked up I was deciding between trying to explain what I was doing here or clobbering you. You make a very convincing guard."

"I'd better," Carl said. "What next?"

"Go out there and get that officer to walk around this corner," Chester instructed him.

"How?"

"I don't know. You're the corporal. Say something that will get yon gray-clad officer off his duff and around this corner. I'll take care of the rest."

"OK," Carl said doubtfully. "Let me think for a moment." He paused and considered, drawing on his lifetime of military experience to come up with a statement that would draw the officer away from his companions. Then he strode out to the table around which the gray-uniformed soldiers were sitting.

"Good morning, sir," Carl said, snapping an informal salute. "The Adjutant would like to see you in his office. He sent me to escort you."

The gray-clad officer looked up lazily and returned

the salute. "Adjutant?" he asked. "Adjutant? I didn't know you people had an adjutant."

"Yes, sir," Carl said. He offered no further explanation, but just waited silently.

"Do you know what it might be about?" the officer asked.

"No, sir," Carl said.

"Oh, well," the officer sighed. "More administrative details." He turned to the civilian. "If you will excuse me, sir?"

"Of course, of course," the civilian said. "But I tell you, Colonel Nottoway, these persons are more trouble than they're worth. More trouble."

"You're the one that makes the money in dealing in these persons," Colonel Nottoway said. "I'd much prefer to be up north on the line with my troops."

"I didn't make the regulations, Colonel," the civilian said. "I'm just as much a slave of them as you are."

"Perhaps," the colonel said. He gestured toward the men being shackled in the middle of the field. "But not as much as those—persons—there. That right, Mr. Effingham?"

Effingham gave a heavy chuckle that shook his portly frame. "That's right, Colonel. Indeed, sir, that is correct."

Colonel Nottoway rose. "Lead on," he said to Carl. "I'd like to get this business completed as soon as possible."

"Yes, sir," Carl said. "So would I, sir, believe me." He led the way around the corner, and Colonel Nottoway followed.

As they disappeared from the view of the colonel's companions, Chester stepped out from the side of the building. "Excuse me, sir," he said.

"Well, what is it?" Colonel Nottoway demanded, staring distastefully at the prison-garbed scarecrow.

"I just want to hear you speak, sir," Chester said, respectfully. "Idiom, accent, and the like."

"What do you mean?" the colonel said impatiently. "Get out of my way, man."

"You think you're someone in that fancy uniform, don't you, sir?" Chester said. "The aura of self-importance fairly radiates from you. I'd say you're a man used to having his own way. Is that right?"

Colonel Nottoway was obviously puzzled by the dichotomy presented by the man in front of him, blocking his way. He looked like a prisoner, but wasn't awed by authority. The most insulting words came out of the man's mouth in the most respectful tones. The colonel didn't understand. This was the impression Chester was looking for. If the colonel were insufficiently impressed, he would just walk by; if he were overly frightened, he would call for help.

"I am used to having my own way, that's true," the colonel said. "I command a brigade of troops in my sector, some three thousand men, none of whom would dare accost me as you have just done. If you have a point, make it; otherwise get out of my way."

"That should be sufficient, thank you, Colonel," Chester said, stepping aside to allow the colonel to pass.

The colonel sniffed and took two steps. Then Chester clopped him neatly by the side of the head with a sock filled with dirt, and the colonel fell neatly on his face.

"He'll never understand," Chester said, stripping the colonel's uniform off. "He'll think we did it just to humiliate him, the poor man."

Carl went back around the corner and approached the sergeant. "The colonel wants you," he said.

"Where is he?" the sergeant asked.

"Right around there," Carl said. "I'd better take you."

"Excuse me, sir," the sergeant said respectfully to Mr. Effingham. "Be right back, sir."

"Of course," Effingham said, impatiently waving him away. Clearly he didn't bother with sergeants.

Carl led the way around the corner, and Chester knocked the sergeant cold with no preliminaries. "Two out of three," he said. "Not bad."

"I have no idea of how to get that civilian out of his chair," Carl said.

"Know his name?" Chester asked.

"Effingham."

"Fine. Let me handle him. You just concentrate on getting this sergeant's uniform off his back and onto yours as quickly as possible. Then roll him under the barracks with his boss." Chester straightened up and adjusted the dress sword at his waist. "How do I look?"

"Like my daddy told me," Carl said, "clothes do make the man. You look every inch the officer. But Effingham is going to know you're not Colonel Nottoway."

Chester glared at him. "Of course," he said. "There are, after all, other colonels." He walked casually around the side of the building and over to the civilian. "Mr. Effingham?" he inquired.

Effingham looked up and then did a double-take. "Yes?" he said. "Who are you?"

"Arthur's the name. Colonel Chester A. Arthur. May I sit?"

"Of course, of course." Manners came to Effingham's aid, and he nodded the colonel to a seat. "I didn't know any other representatives of the Confederacy were here now. What are you doing here, if I may ask?"

"On business much the same as your own, Mr. Effingham," Chester said. "That's what is causing the problem. It seems there is a question as to just who has prior claim to those men out there." Chester waved a negligent hand.

"You mean the persons being prepared for transport?" Effingham asked. "The ones in the field?"

"The very ones in front of us," Chester said.

"But that's impossible," Effingham said, his voice rising. "I have documentation and authorization from the highest authority...."

"I'm sure we can get it amicably straightened out," Chester said. "I will, of course, bow to higher authority if you have such documentation."

"I can assure you, sir—" Effingham began, rising from his seat in agitation.

"No need, no need," Chester said, also rising. "We'll merely show your documentation to the Adjutant, and I'll wait for the next batch. Let's get it straightened out now." He strode toward the fatal corner, and Effingham came after like a carp rising to the bait.

10

The three bogus representatives of the Confederacy waited impatiently for the island authorities to finish preparing the prisoners for transport. Now that the shackles were in place, two men were going down the line of prisoners dying their faces and hands black; a time-consuming process.

"What's that for?" Carl asked. "Make them easier to spot?"

"Harder for them to escape," O'Malley said.

"It's the tradition," Chester told them. "Apparently on Earth at this time a race of black people were slaves of this group called the Confederacy. They were put to work picking cotton. The country to the north, called the Union, wanted to free these blacks so they could come up north and work in the factories. So they had a war."

"Another war," Carl said. "Is that the only thing in Earth history—war?"

"It's the only thing worth watching, just about," Chester said. "Or at least that's what the fives think."

"If they find any of our friends which we've left lying about before we get out of here," O'Malley said, "we'll have a nice little war of our own here."

"Let us hope that doesn't happen," Chester said.

One of the guards trotted up to the group and saluted. Then he got a good look at them, and frowned. "Are you the Confederate gentlemen I escorted here?" he asked.

"I don't know," Chester snarled. "All you people look alike to me. Is that group ready for transport?"

"Yes, sir," the guard said, still looking puzzled.

"I'll inform Colonel Nottoway as soon as he gets back from the Adjutant's office," Chester said.

"Yes, sir," the guard said, looking relieved. There was a rational explanation. His was not to reason why, anyway. "The forms have to be signed."

"Of course they do," Chester agreed. "Hand them over."

"Yes, sir." The guard handed him a clipboard with a variety of varicolored forms attached to it. "On the bottom line on the green ones," he said. "Anywhere on the red ones. Just initial the pink master sheet. And sign the blue one where it says 'I accept delivery of the items enumerated on this form.'"

Chester signed *Chester A. Arthur, Colonel, Army of the Confederacy*, wherever he could find a spot. "There," he said. "Can we take them away now?"

"In a few minutes, sir," the guard said. "Someone will come for you." He saluted again and trotted away.

"He knows!" O'Malley whispered urgently. "Did ye hear what he said? 'Someone will come for ye!' No doubt!"

He didn't impress me as being that subtle," Chester said. "Just relax. We'll be on our way in a couple of minutes."

It seemed like an hour before another guard headed in their direction, but it probably was only a couple of minutes. This one didn't seem to have any preconceived notion of what they should look like; he was perfectly happy with them as they were. "If you'll come this way, gentlemen, please," he said, "we're about ready to load."

He took them into the guardhouse, through a series of corridors, and into a large room. A minute later the shackled persons were led into the room. Then the door closed, and the room began to descend into the ground.

Carl's first reaction was panic, a feeling that apparently many of the prisoners shared. They began shrieking and jumping up and down, to the extent that their leg shackles would permit.

One of the guards had obviously experienced this reaction before, and knew just how to reassure his charges. "All of you just shut up and stand still," he said, hefting his club in his hands, "or I'll take the wind out of you with the point of my billy." This had a strong calming effect on the prisoners, especially after he demonstrated on one man and left him doubled up in a corner, retching and gasping for air.

"I'd like to speak to that lad sometime," O'Malley said, in a violent whisper to Carl and Chester. His doubled-up right fist beat spasmodically against his left palm.

"I hate to take your mind away from pleasures of the flesh," Chester said in an undertone, "but we have more important considerations right now. Do nothing to attract attention."

"Aye," O'Malley agreed sourly.

The elevator reached the bottom of its passage, and the big doors opened again. They were on the train platform, and the train waited in front of them: a great, windowless, black slug, segmented down its length by shiny metal bands. The doors opened as they watched, sliding upward into the body of the train. The interior glowed with a slightly greenish light.

"Residents to the left, hurry now," the lead guard said, starting the line of prisoners out of the elevator.

"That would put us to the right, I would imagine," Chester said. They waited for the file of prisoners to pass, and then walked over to the open train door to the right of the elevator.

The door was so low that even O'Malley had to stoop over slightly to enter the car. The interior held two rows of benches along the sides of the car, broken only for the doors. The benches had molded depressions for the individual seats, which were further segregated by short metal bars that jutted out from the side of the car and served as handrails. The green light came from concealed panels in the walls of the car.

They were alone in the car. O'Malley settled into one of the seats opposite the open door. "We'll never get off this train alive, ye realize," he said pleasantly. "They'll be waiting for us at the other end with instructions to shoot on sight."

"Don't be a pessimist," Chester told him.

"Pessimist!" O'Malley said. "Why, that's the optimistic viewpoint. What will probably happen to us is too frightful to think about. I have a sense of deep foreboding."

Two guards got on and settled across the car from them. One of the guards pulled a leatherbound book from his pouch bag and started reading, and the other took some large copper coins from his pocket and practiced palming them and moving them across the tops of his fingers. Neither paid any attention to the three Confederates.

"Ye see," O'Malley whispered, "it's a plant! They're on to us."

"Shut up!" Chester mouthed, as the reading guard glanced curiously over at them. "You see," he continued in his normal tone, "the structure of this car is very interesting, and tells much about the people who designed it."

The door slid down and sealed, and the train lurched gently to a start.

"They were shorter and squatter than humans, for one thing," Chester continued, "as is evidenced by the height of the door and the width of these seats."

"Yes, Colonel," Carl said in a respectful tone as befits a sergeant, "and is there anything else?"

"They did not originate on this planet, but were visitors much as we are," Chester said. Both guards were interested now, and their looks were guileless and free of suspicion.

"Your pardon, sir," the book reader said, leaning forward across the aisle. "This is a subject that is of interest to me. Why do you say that the elder race, the builders of this underground railway, were not of this planet?"

"Simple and easily explained," Chester said. "The lighting that permeates this room is green and not white. The sun around which we revolve gives, to our eyes, a perfectly white light; which means it is of the same spectral class as the sun under which our race evolved.

"These people, whoever they were, evolved around a cooler sun, and the center of their visible spectrum was shifted into the green. It is also possible that a difference in the composition of their home-world atmosphere, and the light it would let through, was responsible. At any rate, it was not this world."

"That seems perfectly clear, sir," Carl said, resolving to have Chester explain at the earliest opportunity what some of those words meant. It was obvious that insufficient education was a serious handicap.

"I don't mean to dispute you, sir," the guard said. "But find your reasoning interesting, and would like to pursue the logic to the ultimate conclusion. Is it not possible that the builders of this train merely found the green light more stimulating, or conversely more relaxing, than natural light? On the other hand, could it not be that the light panels themselves, over the course of the many years since the elder race disappeared, have shifted up in frequency until they are centered below the blue, and thus appear green to our eyes?"

Chester thought this over. "Possible," he admitted, "but improbable. One does not wish to attempt to predict the thought processes of an alien mind, but I find it hard to imagine why one would wish to stimulate the necessarily passive riders of a subway during their journey. Conversely, would not the passengers who found it necessary to conduct some business on the train—writing perhaps, or reading, assuming they did such—complain about relaxing lighting that made it harder to accomplish their ends? Do you not find it difficult to read under this green light?"

"I do, sir, you are right," the guard admitted.

"As to the light panels shifting spectrum over the course of years, would we not find, then, that some had shifted more than others due to slight inconsistencies in the manufacture? And yet they all seem to glow with the same brightness and constant hue. Thus it seems to me that they are as they were when installed long years ago."

The guard nodded. "Thank you, sir," he said. "You have given me much to think about."

They lapsed into silence, and the guard resumed his book. The train continued on its way with unabated, if unknown, speed.

After a while the two guards began a soft argument between themselves about the relative merits of day shift versus night shift, and Carl ventured a quiet question to Chester. "What is the plan, sir, when we arrive?"

"We reconnoiter as rapidly as possible, and then we disappear," Chester told him.

"Sounds good," Carl agreed. "Sir."

"That's right, keep up the front, Carl, my boy," Chester said. "I am your superior officer as long as we're in these uniforms. It adds an air of verisimilitude to our otherwise bald and unconvincing narrative."

The train slowed to a stop and opened its doors.

Neither of the guards moved, so Chester signaled his two companions to keep their seats, and they nervously waited for the doors to close again.

Chester leaned forward. "I would like to survey this station," he told the guard with the book. "How long will the doors be open?"

"If you stay put, about five minutes," the guard told him. "If you get out, they will slam closed behind you."

"Curious," Chester said.

"It's the automatic machinery," the guard told him, "operating by an alien logic."

The doors dropped closed, and the train started again. "I wonder how many more stops before we get off?" Carl whispered. "And I wonder if we get off at the same stop as the guards?"

"An interesting question," Chester admitted. "We shall have to watch carefully for cues."

The train went on. Time passed, and Carl wished that he had a book to read. A textbook on infantry tactics, perhaps, although it looked like that would never be useful to him again. That phase of his life was clearly over. He would never be a knight. His father would have to be happy with his pension, if they didn't cut it off when they discovered that Carl had escaped.

Carl sat brooding about it, and felt a terrible sense of injustice. Not at his present situation, but at his past. His whole life had been a lie. He had not only been a prisoner all his life, but he hadn't even known it. Now, for the first time, on this train, with the threat of capture or death a few hours off, he was free. His destiny was, for the first time, his own, if he were clever and fast enough to stay in front of his pursuers.

The train stopped and the door slid up. Carl tensed, watching the guards. They stood up and nodded to their fellow passengers. "Good-bye!" the book reader said. "Give our regards to Atlanta, next stop." And the two of them left the train, carefully ducking through the low door.

"Well," Chester breathed, and his shoulders sagged. "Thank the Lord for small favors. Now we know where to get off."

The door dropped shut, and the train started off again.

"Atlanta?" O'Malley asked. "Where's that?"

"In the heart of the Confederacy," Chester told him. "And only two sectors over from Sanloo."

Carl continued his brooding as the train went on. This time his thoughts turned to Alyssaunde. Why had she left him? He felt particularly betrayed. Even if there were nothing she could do about his imprisonment, she could have at least come to see him. Well, she was a five and he was an ex-corporal-turned-prisoner, and what could she care about him?

"How do we proceed?" O'Malley asked Chester.

"In a westerly direction," Chester said. "And cautiously. It would be silly to attempt to make plans, for we have no idea of what lies ahead. We must just stick together and use our heads. And remember, O'Malley, no precipitous action. If you have one minute to act in, spend the first thirty seconds planning—then move fast."

"My scheme exactly," O'Malley agreed.

"Hm," Chester said. "I hadn't noticed."

The train slid to a stop and the door lifted. Carl peered out at the great tile station. A wooden sign had been erected against one wall that read: ATLANTA— PERSONS DEPOT.

"What is this 'persons' business?" Carl asked.

"That is what the Confederates call their black-faced workers," Chester said. "It dates back to an ancient document of some sort." He waved his hand at the wide station. "Shall we?"

"We'd best, before the door closes," O'Malley said. "Who knows where we'd end up then."

They stepped off the train, and the door immediately dropped behind them.

❊ 11 ❊

The "persons" were being led off the back car. The guards turned them over to a group of waiting gray-clad soldiers, who lined them up and inspected them. One of the soldiers approached the trio and stopped in front of Chester. "Are you the accompanying officer?" he asked, performing a casual salute.

"I am," Chester snapped. "Is that the way you usually salute a superior officer?"

"No, sir," the soldier said, snapping to attention. "Sorry, sir." He gave a crisp salute.

The soldier didn't seem particularly surprised or resentful, Carl noted. Evidently officers were officers regardless of the period or culture.

"Will you sign this please, sir?" the soldier requested, thrusting a clipboard in Chester's face.

Chester surveyed the document on the board, studied it closely for a minute, then scribbled something illegible on it at the bottom with Colonel Nottoway's pen. "Here you are, son," he said, handing it back.

"Thank you, sir," the soldier said, tendering a second crisp salute, doing a perfect about-face, and stalking back to his companions.

"We'd best let those lads and their charges go up first," Chester said. "I don't think he'll be particularly anxious to wait for me."

They stood there while the elevator door closed and it started to ascend, with a faint whooshing noise.

"Say," Carl said, approaching the door and staring at it. "How do we call it back?"

"I have no idea," Chester told him. "Let us hope that some notion presents itself."

The three of them examined the door minutely, looking for some lever, button, switch, pushplate, or other device for recalling the elevator, but could find nothing. "Very clever," O'Malley sighed. "I knew in my heart it would end like this."

"What end?" Chester asked, looking down at his friend.

"We're stuck here until they come for us," O'Malley said. "Which will be soon, I have no doubt."

"Ever the cheery disposition," Carl said. "Surely there must be stairs."

Something said *merp!*

"What was that?" Carl demanded, backing up.

"I have no idea," Chester said, grabbing the hilt of his borrowed presentation sword and half drawing it from its scabbard.

The elevator door opened.

"Ye worry too much," O'Malley said, stepping into the empty elevator. "Ye should be like me, and cheerfully trust in the fates to take care of ye. Ever optimistic, that's what I am."

Chester and Carl followed him into the elevator, and the door closed behind them. "Hm," Chester said. "Voice operated, perhaps; or sensitive to body heat; or aware of motion by the door? Fascinating." He dropped his sword back into the scabbard.

When the elevator opened at the top of its journey, they faced a long corridor which went off in front of them. There was no one in it, and it was bare except for an occasional door that opened to the left, and one great pair of doors that went off to the right.

"I have a feeling," Chester said as they got off, "that the large doors are where they take the 'persons,' so we should pick one of the others."

"Which one?" Carl asked.

Chester shrugged. "Flip a coin," he said.

"There are six doors," Carl said.

"So flip a six-sided coin," Chester snapped. "Look—" He pulled a copper from his pocket. "First flip, left three or right three." He flipped it. "Tails: right three. Now, to be perfectly fair, I shall flip it three times, odd door out." He flipped, and it came down head-tail-head. "Middle door of the right three," he said.

"If there's anything I admire," Carl said, "it's the way your incisive logic cuts to the heart of any situation."

Chester paused to glare at him. "Is that any way for a sergeant to speak to his colonel?" he demanded.

"Sir," Carl amended.

"That's better. Now, forward! And try to look like we know what we're doing, whatever we find on the other side of that door."

The door had a curious square handle, and opened easily at their touch. On the other side was a vast hall with a low ceiling, and many waist-high booths scattered in some haphazard manner throughout its area.

The door closed behind them when they were through, and Carl noticed that there was no handle on the outside. He pointed this out to Chester.

"More interesting than that," Chester said, "look to your left."

Carl looked to the left, on the other side of the wall they had just come through, and saw that all four of the other doors also came through to this vast hall. He turned to the right, and saw that the last one also came out here. "Well," he said. "I wonder why that should be. Our aliens had curious minds."

"I think this is a human construction," Chester said. "This whole building was built by the authorities, whether of just this sector, or planetary, I don't know, to hide the existence of the subway entrance."

"Then why the six separate doors?" Carl asked.

"To help hide the elevator entrance. It looks like they lead to six separate places. A subtle design."

The room they had entered was very busy and quite noisy. People clustered about the various booths and ran from booth to booth. There was a lot of arm-signaling going on, and cryptic signs were being wigwagged back and forth at the tips of fingers. The atmosphere was cluttered but very purposeful, and everyone seemed to know why he was there and what he was doing. There were, as far as Carl could tell, no women present anywhere in the room.

Each of the booths had a sign up, and the signs varied greatly in size and construction, but there was a certain sameness in the wording:

ARTHUR SCHULEYER SONS & COMPANY
FIELDHANDS AND DECKHANDS
EXPERIENCED AND NOT
P.E. License # 103

THE GREAT SOUTHERN CORPORATION, LTD.
PERSONS FOR EXPORT
NO PERSON TOO OLD OR TOO WEAK
P.E. License #58

WALLACE & LEE
FEMALE PERSONS
GENTLED
SUITABLE FOR HOUSEWORK
BONDED—THE OLD FIRM
P.E. License #23

Theos: P. Ragg
Specialist in Trained Clerical Persons
Our word is our guarantee
P.E. License # 202

They walked rapidly through the large hall toward what looked to be exits to the outside world. "Don't raise your hand in here," Chester warned, "or you may end up having bought someone."

"They sell people?" Carl asked, a note of disbelief in his voice.

"That's what slavery's all about," Chester said.

"I thought it was, like, the government," Carl said. "Not other people. How can one person own another?"

"Be careful how you use the word 'person' around here," Chester advised him. "And who do you think makes up the government, if not people? And what gives them any more right to own other people than anyone else?"

Atlanta was a moderate-sized town of wooden frame houses, except for the large square concrete building out of which they walked. The street was packed dirt, with wooden sidewalks; and elaborate carriages bounced along on high springs raising clouds of dust as they passed.

The sign above the door they left read:

PERSONS EXCHANGE

Around the back were high, concrete walled pens, in which were stored the persons until they were sold. The persons wore one-piece coveralls of blue denim, much like prison garb except for the color, and black hands and faces, and leg shackles.

The gentlemen of the sector, ascending and descending carriages and attending to the business of the exchange, were garbed in dark gabardine suits with figured vests and tall stovepipe hats. They looked elegant, almost effete, and untouched by the business in which they were engaged. Many of them wore fancy high boots with designs tooled and stained into the leather.

Chester watched them strut in and out of the Persons Exchange for a long minute with a curious expression on his face. "'Their uniforms were spick and span,'" he muttered:

"'And they wore their Sunday suits,
But we knew the work they had been at,
By the quicklime on their boots.'"

"What's that?" Carl asked.

"A bit of ancient verse," Chester explained. "No matter."

"Let us make our way away from here," O'Malley said. "I don't fancy the smell."

"Look!" Carl said, indicating an object high in the sky to his right.

"A flitterboat," Chester said. "And, if I'm not mistaken— Yes, a Guest flitter, and not an Inspector's craft."

"We're back in civilization, that we are," O'Malley said. "And back on display."

"We'd better get away from here," Chester said, "and get out of these clothes. It's not going to be too many more hours before the word is out. We'll probably be hunted by the Inspectors and the local police and the military."

"You make life sound so interesting," Carl said.

"Ye're a delightful man to travel with," O'Malley agreed. "And if it's traveling we should be doing, then which way should we be doing it?"

"Unless I am mistaken," Chester said, "that large structure about two blocks down is a train station. The trains won't be as comfortable or modern as the one we just left, but perhaps we can get one going in the right direction."

Several more flitterboats came into view, hovering above the city. "Those things make me nervous," Carl complained."

"Don't worry about the Guests," Chester said. "They're no more interested in you than you are in them. They just go where the excitement is."

"That's what I'm worried about," Carl said. "What are they doing here?"

Chester paused to consider. "An interesting thought," he said. "They get lists each morning, you know, telling what is going to be happening where. And they do seem to be congregating here. Let's get to the station with reasonable speed, shall we?"

The flitterboats were gathering over Atlanta, but they didn't seem to favor any one section of the city over any other. "We may be in for an attack," Chester said. "Listen, if we get separated, we meet in Sanloo at a place called the Fat Black Pussycat. You know how to cross the barrier."

"Aye," O'Malley agreed dourly.

"I don't," Carl said.

"Ye'd best stick with one of us, then," O'Malley said. They walked down the street at a brisk pace, but not fast enough to attract undue attention, toward the building Chester thought was a train station.

There was a tremendous crash from somewhere behind them, and then the sound of yelling and running feet. And then the screaming started: shrill, hysterical screams that built in intensity and volume and then suddenly cut off.

"What under the two moons—!" O'Malley said. They turned around, and saw nothing different in the street behind them. The carriages had mostly pulled to a halt, and the drivers and passengers were also looking around, trying to locate the yelling.

Like a flood of water newly released from a broken dam, a horde of black-faced prisoners rounded the building and ran into the street. Most of the prisoners were free of their leg irons, but some were still shackled together in groups of five or six. They held a variety of weapons, from hunks of chain to broken-off sections of pipe, and they threatened or attacked everyone they came in contact with. Most of the gentlemen had walking sticks, but they were alone and the prisoners were all together. Every time one of the gentlemen went down, another black-faced prisoner gained a weapon.

When they reached the street they overthrew the carriages they could get at, and the air was filled with a great crashing noise. Most of the drivers managed to get their horses turned around before the prisoners reached them, and headed away at high speeds. There were several collisions between escaping carriages, which added to the general confusion.

"By the Big Moon," Chester said, "a slave revolt! I'll bet it's happening all over town. That's the only way it has a chance, so the police can't concentrate in any one spot."

"What about the Inspectors?" Carl asked. "Hadn't we better get away from here?"

"Yes," Chester agreed. "But not because of the Inspectors; this is merely a local thing, and they won't interfere. As a matter of fact, it must have been programmed, since it seems to have been on the Guests' lists."

"That's right!" Carl said. He looked around and saw that the sky was now thick with flitterboats, which were staying at a respectful distance above the confusion below. "And you're right, it must be happening all over the city. At least, the flitters don't seem to be concentrated in any one area."

They were retreating at a respectful speed, staying well ahead of the mass of slaves, when a second group of slaves came around a corner and spotted them. "Soldiers!" the cry went up among the slaves. "Get them!"

"I think it's time for a strategic retreat," Chester muttered. "Head for the railroad station."

Carl broke into an easy dogtrot, which changed

rapidly to a full run when the slave mob took to its collective heels after them. They had a lead of about ten yards, but didn't seem to be making any progress. If anything, the mob was gaining.

"Around this corner," Chester yelled, and the three of them swung around a corner to their left. The mob followed right behind.

Ahead of them, marching out of the dust cloud that was starting to envelope the city, a troop of soldiers marched, their rifles at right shoulder arms, a mounted officer at their head.

"Detachment—halt!" the officer commanded when he saw the slave mob round the corner.

The troop halted and awaited further commands.

"Deploy in two ranks across the street!" the officer commanded, and the troops easily trotted into position.

Chester, Carl, and O'Malley headed straight for the line of troops about thirty yards in front of them, with the mob still on their heels.

"Fix bayonets!" the officer commanded, taking a position on the side of the street from which he could see everything.

Twenty yards now, with the mob only five yards behind and gaining. The sight of the line of riflemen seemed only to enrage them.

"Rifles to the ready!" the officer yelled, and the men put their weapons to their shoulders. There was no question of aiming.

The officer timed it nicely. As the three of them reached the line and entered it, and the nearest of the mob was within five yards of the line, he yelled, "Fire!"

The crash of the rifles deadened all other sound, and their smoke blackened all sight. But as the smoke lifted, the mob reached the line of soldiers, over the bodies of their fallen companions, and attacked in a rage of club and chain against bayonet.

The line broke, and in a second the fight had become a melee, all over the street, man against man in more or less single combat. Chester drew his sword and Carl picked up the rifle of a fallen soldier, and they stood back to back and beat off the black-faced mob. Carl had no experience handling a rifle, but an unloaded rifle with a bayonet on the end is a pike, and he had spent the best years of his life training on the pike.

The smoke and dust were heavy, and they couldn't see what was happening more than about ten feet away from them, but a continuous supply of black faces came out of the smoke and had to be beaten off.

Then the faces stopped coming out of the smoke, and Carl sat down on the ground and breathed heavily. "Well," he said when he had enough breath to speak again. "Nothing like a bit of exercise on a Tuesday afternoon."

"Is it Tuesday?" Chester asked, leaning against a street water fountain and staring down at Carl through reddened eyes. "I had quite lost track."

"Where's O'Malley?" Carl asked.

Chester looked around. "I don't see him," he said. "Wait till the smoke settles, he's bound to be around here somewhere."

The mounted officer was reassembling his troops and surveying his damage. The slaves, those who were not flat on their faces in the street, were gone. Run off singly to reassemble as another mob somewhere else with less professional resistance.

The smoke was clearing, and O'Malley was still nowhere in sight. The officer rode over and saluted Chester. "Captain Duquesne at your service," he said. "Third Infantry, sir."

"Colonel Arthur," Chester said, returning the salute. "And my sergeant and I would like to thank you and your men for your timely assistance."

"Not at all, sir," the captain said. "Our pleasure.

And if you ever feel like lending us your sergeant for a few weeks, we'd be glad to have him. I've never seen bayonet work like that. Could sure use him to teach the men." He saluted again and rode back to where the wounded were being assembled.

"Let's head off to the train station," Chester said. "O'Malley is a sensible man; perhaps he awaits us there."

❊ 12 ❊

They reached the train station without further incident, although parties of troops, civilian vigilantes, and rampaging slaves trotted across their field of vision in the distance. They did nothng to encourage any of the groups to approach them.

The station was ringed with troops, and very busy inside. O'Malley was nowhere to be seen. There was a train leaving almost immediately for Vicksburg, and the station map showed that to be off to the west, up near the barrier, so they boarded.

"Shouldn't we wait for O'Malley?" Carl asked Chester as he hurried him onto the train.

"O'Malley is well able to take care of himself," Chester said, "and he knows where to meet us. When this trouble dies down we're going to have a lot of people looking for us, and they're going to be looking here. So we'd better not be here. The slave revolt may turn out to be a very lucky thing for us, as it's certainly going to delay anything like a search."

They settled into a pair of wicker seats facing each other, and waited for the train to pull out. "Have they any chance?" Carl asked.

"Who?"

"The prisoners—the slaves."

"None," Chester told him. "They have no weapons, no organization, no leaders, and no skill. And, with their faces dyed black, no place to hide."

The train started, jostling them from side to side as

it clicked over points and changed tracks to get on the main line of Atlanta. Then the ride steadied down to a regular, rhythmic bouncing and clicking.

"If the Guests knew about it in advance," Carl said, "then it must have been instigated from outside."

"That's right," Chester agreed. "It's authentic history, there were slave revolts; and it's a good show. The Guests eat things like that up."

"Hundreds of people will get killed," Carl said, "on both sides."

"Probably," Chester agreed.

"We could have been on either side," Carl said. "We could just as easily have ended up as slaves as disguised soldiers."

"Easily," Chester said.

"The slaves don't have a chance," Carl said, "and it's not even their own revolt. There's something wrong with that."

"I'm convinced," Chester said.

"But what can we do?" Carl asked.

"Get off this planet," Chester said. "Find Earth—the real Earth. See if they know what's happening here."

"Perhaps they don't care," Carl said.

"Perhaps they merely don't know," Chester said. "Perhaps we can find somebody who does care. Besides, we can't stay here."

"What a strange thing that is," Carl commented.

"What's that?"

"To look at a whole planet and say, 'We can't stay here.' And, I suppose, to have somewhere else to go."

A quartet of officers came into the car and settled in the next group of seats. One of them had a newspaper under his arm, and they were in hot discussion of one of the items on the front page.

"I say *The Virginia* will sink her in the first exchange," one of them stated firmly.

"I say they'll fight for a week, or until they both

run out of ammunition," another said, "and the only result will be that both crews are stone deaf at the end of the engagement."

"My money says that *The Monitor* will hole *The Virginia*, and her best bet will be to ram," a third offered. "Those Yankees build better naval cannons, and their plate is just as good, but they don't understand the rivet! And that could make the difference, properly handled."

The fourth officer shook his head sadly. "You don't understand naval warfare," he said. "The basic problem is that this engagement is being fought at all. There's no rhyme or reason for it. The function of the ironclads isn't to sit out there and bounce cannonballs off each other. They should each ignore the other, and go about their primary task of sinking the wooden hulls. If *The Virginia* could keep away from *The Monitor* for four months, she could have the Yankee blockade broken; and that's vastly more important than sinking the Northern ironclad."

"You think *The Monitor* would allow *The Virginia* to just steam about sinking Northern ships?" the third asked. "No, the battle must be joined, and upon the outcome, I tell you, gentlemen, hinges the fate of the war."

"Come on," the first one said, "the Confederate States have been fighting the Union for over three hundred years now. You don't really think that one little battle between two ships is going to make that much difference. After all, *The Virginia* and *The Monitor* have met before, and nothing decisive has happened yet."

"What I wish," the third one said, "is that I had a friend who was a Guest or an Inspector. I sure would love to get a bird's-eye view of the battle. I'll bet the flitters will be out in force for it."

"Hush!" the first one said, glancing nervously around. "Don't talk like that."

"Come on," the third one laughed, "there's nobody here but the army." He turned around to face Chester. "What do you think, sir, if you'll excuse me?"

"Perfectly all right, Captain," Chester said. "What do I think about what?"

"Them, ah, the ironclads, sir," the first one nervously interjected. "What do you think of the coming battle of *The Monitor* and *The Virginia?*"

Chester eyed them severely. "Gentlemen," he said. "Whatever the outcome of this engagement, the war will be won or lost by the infantry. This is principally a land war, gentlemen, and it is up to the infantry, with the aid of the cavalry and the artillery, to bring it to a conclusion."

"Of course, of course," Captain Number One replied, even more nervously, suddenly realizing that this discussion of the merits of two ships would sound almost like treason to an old-line infantry colonel. "I didn't mean—I only meant—"

"Say!" Number Two said. "Let's dash into the dining car and get a snack, what d'ya say?"

And in a few seconds they had all filed out, casting apprehensive glances over their shoulders at Chester as they went through the connecting door.

"You sure know how to clear a room," Carl said.

"We couldn't afford to get friendly with them," Chester said. "They might ask difficult questions, like 'What unit are you with?'"

Carl stared out the window watching the countryside pass by. "We'll have to answer that," he finally said.

"Eh?" Chester responded. "Answer what? You mean about what unit we're with?"

"I mean if somebody asks us that, yes. But what if anybody asks us anything? What kind of answers can we give? What is this war we're in the middle of, for example. What's this whole part of the world like?

How are we going to fit in here, make a place for ourselves?"

The giant Chester leaned forward and tapped Carl on the knee with one heavy finger.

Carl winced. "Ouch!" he said, trying to stifle the exclamation of pain.

"I'm sorry," Chester said.

"It's nothing."

"But listen, my friend," Chester said in a conspiratorial voice, "for the moment we have to keep an attitude of watchful waiting. We're headed for the sector barrier and if we can make it across we'll be in one of the most advanced sectors on the whole planet."

"What about O'Malley?" Carl interjected.

"O'Malley is our wild card. If anything happens to us, he's our outside man. He'll find us somehow. Different and I have been through a lot, Carl, my boy. He may not seem like the most competent fellow around, but he's got more twists to his cerebral cortex than you think. He's always coming up with some startling notion."

"And I suppose he regards us the same way," Carl said. "Wherever he is, if he gets in trouble he expects us to come to the rescue."

"I suppose so."

Carl's stomach gurgled at him. "Say, Chester, do you think we could get something to eat on this train?"

"I suppose so—that's where our naval strategist friends went."

"Maybe one of us should peep into the dining car, then, to see if they're gone yet."

Chester shook his head. "That would look suspicious. Better we go in together. Brazen it out, my boy."

They stood up and made their way through the swaying, creaking car. The seats were crowded with travelers in and out of uniform, soldiers headed back to their units from leave at home (and vice versa), old men and women, merchants and businessmen. The countryside outside the train was low, rolling hills covered with trees and tall grasses. When the train passed a farm he could see horses and farm equipment. It was a beautiful world, Carl told himself—if only it were real.

Well, it was real for them! There might be some sort of artificial structure imposed on it, some mysterious pattern understood only imperfectly by the fives and not at all by the rest of the people. Something that the Guests knew about. If only he could have talked with Alyssaunde! She was the only person he'd ever met who seemed to understand everything that was happening—but that opportunity was past; he would never see her again in all likelihood.

As the train jolted around a curve in the tracks Carl saw Chester's huge back disappear through the doorway into the dining car. Carl followed. Unlike the passenger coaches, the dining car was relatively deserted. The four officers he'd seen earlier were still sitting at a table. A black-faced person was hovering near them, pouring coffee when cups were emptied. One of the officers had produced a bottle of some brownish beverage and added it from time to time to the cups of coffee.

The senior of the four—a yellow-haired, bronze-skinned man wearing major's insignia on his epaulettes—looked up and smiled at Chester and Carl. Carl saw Chester acknowledge his grin with a wave of the hand.

A second black-faced person emerged from the kitchen compartment at the end of the car and obsequiously ushered Carl and Chester to a table. They sat down and ordered food. The servant hustled away to fetch it for them.

"It's a good thing they permit officers and enlisted

men to dine together hereabouts," Chester muttered to Carl. "In some armies we'd have had to separate."

"Chester," Carl said, "I'm pretty uncomfortable with those four so nearby. What if they recognize us as fakes?"

"Don't worry, my boy. It's almost certain not to happen. But if it does—Different O'Malley and I have been through tighter scrapes than that would amount to. We'll make it to the barrier all right, and into the next sector."

"And when we get there? What then?" Carl demanded.

Before Chester could answer the servant was at their elbows putting down cups of hot soup and dishes with their food. Chester had ordered a couple of lamb chops that came with little frilly paper pants to keep the diner's fingers clean. Carl had ordered beefsteak, a dish he'd had only a few times in his life. He might die tomorrow, but today he would dine!

When the servant disappeared Chester said quietly, "Carl, my boy, when we cross the barrier you will see sights your eyes will hardly credit. Why, the same to you, sir!" The last was spoken with a forced grin. Carl looked where Chester was looking and saw that the blond major was staring curiously at them. Chester reached down with one hand and unobtrusively checked his saber. Carl could see that it was loose in its scabbard. "A mere precaution, my boy," Chester whispered to Carl. "It's too bad that you are not armed. Be ready to use your knife if you must."

Carl swallowed a piece of gristle that forced tears from his eyes. He gulped some of his soup to clear his throat. He could see the four officers—aside from the blond major there were two captains, one fat and soft looking, the other with a lean and hungry look to him, and a very fuzzy-cheeked young lieutenant—engaging in a low-pitched conference.

"I hope they're still just talking about ships," Carl

said to Chester. "But I kind of have my doubts." He looked at the four. The major was staring at Chester harder than ever, and the other three were casting suspicious glances at Chester and Carl.

Finally the major stood up, took a swig at his cup of coffee-and-whatever, and started down the aisle toward Carl's and Chester's table. As he reached it the train swayed suddenly and the major lost his balance. Carl managed to catch him before he crashed into the food and crockery, and shoved him back to his feet.

"Thank you, Sergeant," the major muttered. His speech was somewhat slurred. He turned toward Chester. "If I might have a word with you, sir," the major said.

Chester said, "Of course, Major. What can I do for you?"

"My colleagues and I were admiring your sword, Colonel. Ah, Colonel—I don't believe I caught your name, sir."

"Colonel Nottoway," Chester said.

"Yes, sir. As I said, my colleagues and I were admiring the colonel's sword."

"Yes, thank you." Chester dropped his hand to the hilt of the weapon. "It was a presentation."

"Yes, sir, I recognized that at once, sir."

"And—?" Chester asked.

"It was our outfit that presented it to you, sir, only, if you'll excuse me, sir"—here the major lurched up against the far side of the car and took a minute to straighten himself out—"it wasn't you, sir. If you know what I mean, sir."

"No, Major, I'm afraid I don't," Chester said, smiling up at him.

"You are not the Colonel Nottoway we presented that sword to, sir," the major announced in a loud, clear voice, "and I'm afraid I'm going to have to ask to see your identification, sir. I'm afraid I must insist, sir."

TOMORROW KNIGHT

All noises, Carl noted, slowly came to a stop in the dining car: the cutlery ceased to clatter, saucer stopped clanking against cup, and the hum of conversation died out, as every eye in the car was turned to watch the little drama being played out between Chester and the major.

"Of course, Major," Chester said in a hearty voice. "I would do the same in your place. It's an honest mistake, easily rectified, and I can only commend you for your thoroughness."

"Your identification, Colonel," the major demanded. His three companions got up and clustered around the table.

"Of course, Major," Chester said, digging into his pocket. "The sword you gave was to Colonel *Charles* Nottoway, my cousin. I am"—he glanced quickly into the identification folder as he flipped it open— "Colonel Aubrey Nottoway. We have often remarked, Charles and I, over the amazing similarity between our two presentation blades."

"It was Aubrey Nottoway we gave that sword to, Colonel," the major said, his voice rising an octave and several decibels. "And he ain't you! Where'd you get this sword and that identification folder?"

Chester looked around nervously. "Keep your voice down, Major," he said. "You can never tell who's listening." He leaned forward. "I didn't want to tell you this, but now I suppose I'll have to," he said in a low voice. "I am *not* Colonel Charles Nottoway."

The major signaled over his shoulder to the three companions he had left at their table. But he kept his eyes fixed on Chester A. Arthur all the time. Carl saw the two captains and the fuzzy-cheeked lieutenant put down their cups and make their way down the aisle to stand behind their major.

"I don't believe that you are any Colonel Nottoway, mister," the major said to Chester. "Not Charles, Aubrey, or—"

Chester was on his feet towering over the major. Carl pushed away from the table, mourning over the steak which he now figured he'd never get to eat, and clambered to his feet. "Major, as Colonel Nottoway's aide, sir, I think I can explain. The colonel suffered a head wound some time ago and—"

"You be silent, Sergeant!" the major hissed. "Now both of you two raise your hands high and don't make any sudden moves!"

The three officers clustered behind the swaying major had all pulled weapons from various parts of their clothing and were pointing them menacingly at their newly taken prisoners. Which, Carl realized, was exactly what he and Chester were: prisoners once again. His life, which until the encounters with Alyssaunde had been a well-ordered and rewarding climb through the military ranks of Hiram VI's forces spiced with the excitement of their battles with the Saracens, had turned into a nightmare series of imprisonments, escapes, flights, and recaptures.

The weapons that the two captains and the lieutenant were pointing were only vaguely familiar to Carl. He'd seen fowling pieces in his lifetime: these hand-held weapons were clearly firearms of some related sort. He stared at them, uncertain as to how, precisely, they worked. But he knew that they were built to propel a missile violently from their barrels, one of which was pointing straight at his belly while the other two were directed at Chester.

The lean captain of the pair had shouted instructions to the few other diners scattered through the car, sending them back to their coaches where they would doubtless have wonderful tales to tell their companions. Then the lean captain raised his weapon so that it pointed directly into Chester's face. "Don't you move a muscle, mister, or I'll blow your brains right out the back of your skull! Now, colleague, would you please take Colonel Nottoway's sword away from this man."

The fat captain gingerly drew the sword from its scabbard and slipped it through the decorative belt that circled the waist of his uniform coat.

The major had swayed against the wall of the car, and made his way to a vacant table where he sat now, quietly surveying the scene between his three subordinates and Chester and Carl. "Bring 'em over here," the major called to the captain whose handgun was still pointed straight at Chester's forehead.

The captain gestured and Chester made his way to the major's table, followed by Carl. They sat down facing the major. The two captains, corpulent and lean, seated themselves to either side of the major. The lieutenant—Carl turned his head to make sure and turned it back when he saw the look on the lieutenant's face—stayed standing behind the two prisoners, pointing two guns now. Carl looked at the major and the two captains and decided that the fat captain must have given his gun to the lieutenant.

"The court will come to order," the major announced solemnly.

"Court?" Carl yelped.

"Silence!" the major commanded. Carl could feel the muzzle of a handgun press briefly against the back of his neck. Its metal was hard and cold and he could almost feel a hot projectile splattering through his spine.

"I must protest, Major," Carl heard Chester say. "This is completely irregular. You have no authority over the sergeant and myself, and furthermore you cannot try an officer of grade superior to your own. Now if there is any problem here that can't be worked out among ourselves, let us proceed to Vicksburg and consult the provost marshal."

"Mister," the major said, "that would all make sense

if you were really Colonel Nottoway, but you ain't. As far as I know you are a Union spy and this so-called sergeant of yours is your accomplice. Now you are formally charged with spyin' on the Confederate Army, impersonatin' an officer, theft of transportation services from this railroad, and—well, I could think of a few more things but spyin' alone is a hangin' offense so I guess the others would be superfluous, wouldn't they?"

Chester thumped one giant fist on the table. Carl looked up and saw two black faces peering fearfully from behind the partition that separated dining compartment from kitchen. "This is outrageous!" Chester roared. "When General Lee hears about this ridiculous indignity—"

"Enough!" the major snapped. "Unless you care to properly identify yourselves—"

"I am Colonel Nottoway and this is Sergeant Allan, as we have told you all along, Major!"

"Very well, sir! The court will now vote on the charges as stated against one John Doe posing as Colonel Aubrey Nottoway, C.S.A., and one Richard Roe posing as Sergeant Allan, C.S.A. Guilty?"

Carl's eyes popped open and his jaw dropped as the two captains raised their hands. So did the major.

"Any votes for acquittal?" the major asked.

No one raised a hand.

"I protest!" Chester shouted. Carl saw him begin to explode upward from his seat, then crumple forward, sprawling across the tabletop. He moaned, blood running from his head. Carl turned and saw the lieutenant looking pale, one weapon still pointing shakily at Carl, the other bloodied where he had crashed it into Chester's skull.

"Thank you, Lieutenant," the major said. "Captain," he said to the fat officer, "would you please summon the conductor and have him stop the train for a few minutes. We are going to have us a little hangin' right alongside the tracks, and then we will continue our journey to Vicksburg."

Carl moaned and buried his face in his hands.

❊ 13 ❊

The steam engine pulled to a stop and wheezed heavily. Carl and Chester, their hands tied behind them, were prodded off the train; the four officers and two extra captains they had asked to join them stayed right behind. A few civilians had come out between the cars to watch, but the officers had waved them back inside. "This is a military matter," the major had yelled. "You people stay inside. Watch from the windows, if you want."

Chester's face had been washed, and a clean handkerchief wound around his forehead. "Every man, even a Yankee spy, deserves to die with a clean face," the major had decided.

They led their prisoners over to a convenient grove of trees and stood them together, guarded by the lieutenant, while they tried to decide which tree to use for the ceremony.

"I didn't realize that a hanging was such a complex affair," Chester remarked to Carl as they stood shoulder to shoulder.

"You shut up!" the lieutenant barked.

"My, you certainly do take your responsibilities seriously," Chester told him.

"I warned you," the lieutenant said, obviously very nervous and upset about this whole affair.

Chester eyed the lieutenant speculatively. "I wouldn't get too officious, lad," he said gently. "Don't go beyond what the major orders you to do; it won't look good at the court-martial."

"Shut up, I told you," the lieutenant snapped, looking more and more upset. "What court-martial?"

"Surely you realize that the General Staff is going to have to court-martial all of you for hanging a superior officer?" Chester said. "After all, that is mutiny. But it's not your fault, son; you're only obeying orders. I just hope that someone will testify for you at the trial. Perhaps you won't be shot with the rest of them. Twenty years or so from now, you'll be able to laugh at this."

"But you're a spy," the lieutenant said. "It's right to hang spies."

"But that's not for you or your major to decide," Chester said. "I guess I'll have to trust you, son. After I'm dead, you get the secret identification card out of the lining of my wallet and bring it to General Pickett of C.S.A. Intelligence. He'll know what to do with it."

"You mean—"

"Don't ask questions, son, because I'm not allowed to answer them. Just do as I say. It'll help you at the court-martial."

"The court-martial," the lieutenant repeated, looking unhappy.

"You take good care of them, Lieutenant," the major said, "and don't talk to the prisoners. I'm going to get a rope."

Chester twisted to look at Carl and grinned. "They forgot the rope," he said.

Carl nodded. "Things are looking up," he said weakly, trying to smile back and achieving a sick grin.

"That's an unfortunate choice of words," Chester said. "Don't give up hope, we're not dead yet." He gave a sideways glance at the lieutenant, who was staring wistfully off at the train. "General Lee can always get someone else to complete our mission. Whether we live or die, the South goes on. I only hope it's not too late!" He turned suddenly. "Lieutenant, you won't forget what I asked you to do? It's very important, more important than your life or mine."

"No, sir," the lieutenant whispered, "I'll remember!"

The major came trotting back from the train with a heavy braided rope looped in his hands. "We're in luck," he called; "there's enough here to hang 'em both at once!"

Carl felt the blood draining from his face. It is one thing to face an enemy in battle, with the prospect of being killed, and quite another to face the cold-blooded prospect of your imminent and inevitable death by hanging.

The major cut the rope in half, and a captain took each half and started to climb the two selected trees, to tie the ropes to their appointed limbs.

The engine gave two long blasts on the whistle, and the train started up again, slowly puffing its way down the track. The major almost had a temper tantrum. "I told that pigeon-brained engineer, I distinctly told him to wait! How dare he—"

"Maybe there's a train coming up behind, sir," the fat captain offered.

The major allowed himself to be mollified. "It doesn't matter," he said. "We have business here!"

"What are they going to drop from?" one of the two new captains asked.

"What's that?" the major demanded.

"They have to drop from something," the captain explained. "A horse, a cart, a ladder, something; they can't just fly into the noose."

"Don't be snotty, Captain," the major said. "Lieutenant! Go off and find something for these two spies to drop from. And be quick about it!"

"Don't ye move any part of any of ye in any direction," a hoarse voice yelled, "except yer hands straight up. And fast!"

For an instant everyone froze: a tableau called "The Hanging." Then all present whirled around to face the voice.

Different O'Malley was squatting in a gulley some ten yards from the group. On each side of him, peering over the gulley edge at the assembled Confederate officers, was a black-dyed face. In front of him, its snout facing the Confederate officers, was a crank-operated rapid-fire gun on a small tripod mount.

"Where in blazes did you come from?" the major demanded.

"Yon escaping train," O'Malley told him. "Now get yer hands high in the air before I cut ye off at the middle."

The major waved his hands high in the air. "Don't panic, gentlemen," he squeaked; "we still have the upper hand."

"How's that?" O'Malley inquired.

"Most of these men are armed," the major called. "If you start shooting, they are to pull their weapons and shoot your two friends here—and that's an order!" The last was directed at his men, who looked doubtful at this proposition from their hands-high vantage point. "Now you just come up from there with your hands up before we shoot your friends."

"Yes?" O'Malley said. "And then what will ye do?" He sounded interested.

"Didn't you understand me?" the major asked. "We can surely shoot your friends before you get all of us."

"True," O'Malley said. "But then, ye see the only reason I'm not busy shooting all of ye now is that my friends stand in the midst of ye. Now if ye were to shoot them ye'd remove my inhibition, and I'd mow ye down. So stop talking silly and cut my friends loose. Ye there, the one with the blond hair and the beardless face, remove yer knife from its scabbard and unbind my friends. Hop to!"

The young lieutenant took his small sheath knife from its sheath on his belt and cut the ropes tying Carl and Chester.

"Very good," O'Malley said, turning the muzzle of his weapon slightly to discourage a captain who looked as though he were thinking of being courageous. "Now all of ye drop yer various weapons to the greensward. If ye need a little initiative, I'll shoot yon major to get ye started."

"I think we'd better do as he says, men," the major announced, unbuckling his swordbelt and letting it fall to his feet. The rest of the officers followed suit with little argument. After all, having been bested by three men with a rapid-fire weapon is no disgrace.

"Fine," O'Malley said, loudly and clearly, "now take yer boots off."

If he'd started with that, he would have had an immediate rebellion from these Confederate officers, but he had them in the habit of obeying him now and they did so with only a vague muttering of discontent.

"Ye're all sensible, intelligent men," O'Malley told them. "Now I'd appreciate it if ye'd head over to yon railroad and see if ye can catch up with the train."

"Barefoot?" the major asked, incredulously.

"Take yer time," O'Malley said. "Don't rush it."

With much backward glancing and audible muttering, the Confederate officers made it to the railroad tracks and hobbled after the train.

"Beautiful, O'Malley," Chester yelped, rolling around on the grass and thumping it with his fist.

TOMORROW KNIGHT

"'And then what will you do?' Beautiful! Oh, that major's face!"

Carl sat weakly down on the ground and stared up at the sky. He suddenly felt that life was a mystical experience which he had never fully appreciated before. He resolved to pay more attention to each second as it passed, and to recognize that each minute was beautifully different from the one before it and the one after.

"I don't know what ye two would do without me," O'Malley said. "I'll just have to keep following ye around and picking up after ye."

"And delighted we are for you to do it," Chester said. "How did you get here? Come on out of that hole in the ground and introduce us to your two friends."

O'Malley climbed up and pulled his two black-faced comrades with him. "My friends Hadrien and Roger, meet my friends Chester and Carl." Hadrien and Roger shook hands, then excused themselves to go examine the rapid-fire gun.

"Let's hear it," Chester demanded. "You can't just drop in and save our lives without an explanation."

"Which way to the barrier?" O'Malley asked. "We might as well start walking while I'm explaining. We'd better be long gone when yon officers get back here."

"You're right," Chester said. "And if I'm any judge of character, that major will be back with bloodhounds."

"What about your friends?" Carl asked.

"They want to stay," O'Malley assured him. "They just helped me to get their hands on that gun. They're going to hide out in the woods for a month or so until the black dye is worn off, and then head back to Atlanta to take care of some unfinished business of their own."

"Revenge is not a good motive for conducting business," Chester said, stretching his arms and swinging his large torso from side to side, twisting to get the stiffness out. "It leads to sloppy thinking." He dropped down to do a couple of quick pushups.

O'Malley shrugged. "Pick a direction," he said.

"Due west," Chester said. "Which would be"—he stared thoughtfully toward the sun setting where the horizon met the railroad tracks—"somewhat to the right of those tracks; say that way." He pointed off into the high grass.

"Let's go," O'Malley said.

"Bloodhounds?" Carl asked. "Don't you think we'd better do something about the possibility that he *will* bring back bloodhounds?"

"Oh, he will," Chester said. "He's the sort. We start by putting some distance between us and here. Later we'll worry about the fancy tricks."

They waved good-bye to Hadrien and Roger, contentedly taking apart the rapid-fire weapon, and started trekking toward the west.

After a short period of stumbling through the tall grass, they found a track that led in the basic direction they wanted, and fell into a steady walking pace. "OK," Chester said then, "story time. Let's hear it."

"'Tis very simple," O'Malley said. "I saw ye getting aboard the train from the tracks at the far end of the station. So when it came up to me, I pulled myself up on it. I found myself in a baggage car at the end of the train. My companions, the two escaping prisoners, were very annoyed when I swung aboard. They were hiding in the car."

"Were there no baggage handlers or guards in the car?" Carl asked.

"There were," O'Malley told him, "but they were comatose. A stout length of wood in the hands of Hadrien, I believe, had rendered them so.

"My immediate task was to convince my two companions that I was one of them. It was not easy as I knew so little of life on the island, having spent most of my time there hiding out and building that canoe. But after some little while I did so convince them. Then we started rifling the mailbags, more for want of anything else to do than for any purpose. We were sort of half hoping to find some food."

"And you found that cannon," Chester said.

"Aye, we found the cannon. It was a Patterson Model Four Hand-Cranked, Gas-Cocked, Plate-Fed, Fifty Caliber Field-Mounted Ordnance Piece. There were four of them."

"Plate-fed?" Chester asked. "What does a 'plate' look like?"

"I don't know," O'Malley told him. "We never did find any of the ammunition for it."

"You—" For the first time Carl saw Chester look surprised. Carl knew how Chester felt. His own knees suddenly felt weak.

"So when we saw ye being herded off the train like a couple of geese for the slaughter, we rolled off the far side with the weapons, left the other three in the ditch, and scurried with one to a convenient place to wave it at yer oppressors. Then one of my black-faced pals jumped back into the baggage car for a moment and pulled the train alarm to start the train. And it chugged out of sight. We didn't want any of the passengers seeing us rescue ye and come to the officers' aid."

"I thought those alarms stopped the train," Chester said.

"There's one in the last car that signals the engineer to get moving. It's in case there's another train coming up behind, or something. Hadrien knew about it, and he pulled it, and the train left."

Chester shook his head. "Not loaded, huh? Bluffed

them out with an empty gun. How do you like that? How do you like that?"

O'Malley shrugged. "They didn't know it was empty," he said, "and that's what matters. It's what a man thinks is true which controls his actions, not what is really true."

❈ 14 ❈

They trudged for three days, including most of the first night, before they reached the barrier. Three times they crossed streams and did various clever things to elude the possibly following bloodhounds. Once, on the third day, they heard the sound of baying faintly, off in the distance, but by that time the barrier was in sight in front of them.

The barrier was a cleared earth strip about twenty feet wide, with a blue haze running down the center. It was impossible to tell exactly how high the blue haze went, but it couldn't have been too high because flitterboats crossed over barriers with impunity. Still it was clearly high enough to prevent leaping, or even pole-vaulting over.

"What now?" Carl asked, staring at the body of a rabbit that had innocently tried to cross the barrier and now lay dead on the turned earth.

"I used to service these things," Chester said. "It was my first summer job when I was sixteen. It's easy if you know how." He stalked along parallel to the barrier until he came to a metal post about four feet high that was set in the middle of the clearing, and surrounded by the blue haze.

"There's one of these every quarter-mile or so," he told them. "It's the control unit for this section of barrier."

"How do ye get to it?" O'Malley asked.

"It takes steady hands, confidence, and willpower,"

Chester said. "Watch." He stood perpendicular to the post and stretched his hand out to it, through the blue haze, until he could just touch the small silver ball on top of the post.

The silver ball flipped open to the touch, revealing an inset touch panel. "You'll have about ten seconds," Chester said. "When I say go, just walk straight through the barrier."

"Go!"

Carl and O'Malley walked through the barrier, with Chester right behind them. Carl felt it tingle as he stepped out of the haze, but that was all.

"You mean it's that easy?" Carl asked.

"If you know what to do it's that easy," Chester said. "But experimenting is liable to be deadly, remember."

"Where are we now?" O'Malley asked.

"France," Chester said. "During a period known as World War Two. Sanloo is across the next barrier, west of here."

"Another war?" Carl asked. "Don't any of these sectors have anything but wars?"

"That's what the tourists want to see," Chester said, "so that's what they give them. There are a few sectors that aren't wars; small ones where they hold rain dances or make interesting artifacts."

They followed a path through the woods for a long time, then came out into a large, cultivated valley. At the far end of the valley was a small town that made Carl feel right at home. Except for a few small differences, it looked like the small towns in his sector. "Let's head for the town," he said. "Maybe we can talk them into feeding us."

"Ye didn't like the rabbit I spitted and cooked for ye last night?" O'Malley asked.

"It was fine," Carl said. "But that was last night, and this is this afternoon, and we haven't had anything to eat yet today."

"Eating more than once a day is bad for ye," O'Malley pronounced.

"We might just as well head for the town," Chester said. "It lies right across our path anyway. And maybe they will feed us."

"Maybe they could give us a change of clothes, too," Carl said. "I don't know what they wear in this sector, but it sure isn't these uniforms; and if an Inspector happens to flit by, he'll pick us up just by our dress."

"That's true." Chester nodded. "Local peasant garb is the ticket. If we have anything they'll take in trade."

"I fancy they'll take those uniforms," O'Malley said. "Good strong material, heavy weave. Just remove the brass buttons and various devices, and ye've got good heavy work clothes. Just ask them not to wear them for a few days after we leave."

"Worth trying," Chester agreed.

A loud rumbling noise came from their right, and the three of them instinctively flattened themselves against the ground and watched as a mechanical behemoth came around the bend. There were two more identical monsters behind the first. The three passed where they were hiding and headed toward the town. The ground shook as the machines passed.

"What in the world are those things?" Carl said, sitting up and staring after them.

"They're called 'tanks,'" Chester told him.

The three tanks moved from single file to three abreast, facing the town, then stopped. Their engines were turned off, and all was deathly silent.

Suddenly a puff of smoke issued from the first, followed by a loud boom; then from the second, and the third. Three projectiles arced through the air and fell into the small town in the distance. There were curious belching explosions where they hit. Then the tanks fired again, and again.

Then there was a pause to evaluate the effects of their shelling. Thick smoke was coming up from the village, and tongues of red flame could be seen jutting up from the houses. Screams could be heard over the roar of the fires.

Each tank fired two more rounds. Then they backed up precisely, turned around, and methodically headed back up the trail they had come down.

"What was all that about?" Carl asked, staring down at the distant carnage.

"Your guess is as good as mine," Chester said. "But do try to keep your head down until they pass."

Carl, Chester, and O'Malley stayed head down in the grass as the rumbling noise approached them and passed by.

When the tanks reached the spot in the trail closest to the woods, two men darted out of the woods and headed for the lead tank. The tank's machine guns started chattering, but the men were there by then and the guns didn't bear down on them. The men tossed something under the treads of the tank and dived out of the way.

There was a crumpling sound, and the lead tank clanked to a halt. The two behind it backed up a bit and paused, as if trying to decide what to do.

Two more men broke from cover and practiced broken-field running toward the last tank. This time the machine guns hit one of the men, and he jerked backward as though pulled by an unseen giant hand, and crumpled to the ground.

The second man dived under the tank. There was a loud crumpling sound, and the rear tank was still, and the man did not come out.

The middle tank churned its treads to turn sideways and drove out from between its two fallen brothers. When it was about fifteen feet off the road there was a violent explosion that seemed to come from all around it and envelop it, and then a series of sharp crackling sounds came from inside it as its ammunition exploded. The turret actually popped the track and canted to one side. A thin stream of very black smoke rose to the sky.

The two men got up out of the grass, and six more joined them from the woods. They cautiously approached the two tanks that were still but not burning. Two of them climbed up to the turret of each tank, opened the hatch, and pointed their hand weapons inside. A head appeared in the hatch of the rear tank, then a pair of hands, then a thin young man in a black uniform pulled himself up and sat on the lip of the turret. The man up there barked an order at him, and he slowly climbed down the side of the tank to the ground. Two of the men there roughly searched him, then threw him on the ground and tied his hands behind his back with a short piece of wire.

No one came out of the other tank, and no one else came out of the first one, so the men on the turrets cautiously went in, headfirst. After a while they came back out and threw supplies and weapons down to the men below before climbing down themselves.

The eight men gathered around their prisoner, and a long argument began. Carl sat up to watch, and was able to make out some of the words; just enough to get the drift of the discussion. "They want to shoot him!" he reported in amazement.

"Some of them do," Chester said, "and some of them don't."

"But you don't shoot prisoners," Carl insisted.

"*You* don't shoot prisoners," Chester amended.

"What kind of a war is this?" Carl asked. "First those mechanical things steam up and shell a civilian town, and then a bunch of civilians blow them up and argue about shooting one of the men inside."

"Not all sectors are as civilized as your own," Chester told him.

Apparently the men decided not to shoot the

tanker, or perhaps they were just saving him for later, for they stood him on his feet and started him walking in front of them toward the smoking town.

Chester and Carl quickly dropped back to the ground that O'Malley hadn't left, as the men were now headed right toward them. Carl hugged the ground and closed his eyes and tried to remember the words of prayer of his youth.

"Well, hello there, what's this!" A voice above them demanded. Carl rolled over and stared up at the muzzle of a gun and the smiling face behind it. "Good afternoon," he said, sitting up.

"We don't want to interrupt you gentlemen," Chester said. "Don't mind us, just go on your way."

By this time they were surrounded by all eight men, who stared down at them over the barrels of their guns.

"Get up!" a small, stocky, balding man instructed.

Chester rose as though he had intended to all along. "To whom have I the honor of speaking?" he asked.

"Who are you?" the man demanded. "What are those uniforms?"

"Sir," Chester said, "I am an officer in the Army of the Confederate States of America, and this is my sergeant. Colonel Chester A. Arthur at your service, and my orderly, Sergeant Allan. This gentleman is a good friend of mine—"

"O'Malley's the name," O'Malley interrupted. "Different O'Malley. And who are ye, if I may ask?"

"I am Pierre," the stocky man said, "and these"—he swept an arm around to indicate the group—"are Charles, Jacques, Dominic, Bernard, Jules, Michael, and Ambrose. And one Boche driver."

"We can't stay here," Ambrose said. "Shoot them and let's go."

"You can't shoot us, we are neutrals," Chester said firmly.

"The concept eludes me," Pierre told him. "Where

did you come from? You say you are from America; I have heard of America. How did you get here?"

"We're from the next sector over," Chester said. "Through the woods that way. Things are different there."

"You crossed the barrier?" Pierre asked. "You expect us to believe that? What sort of trick is this?"

"No trick," Chester told him. "We are innocent bystanders."

"We are taking this Boche into the town to be executed by the townspeople," Pierre said. "You'd best come with us, and we will decide what do do with you there."

They stood up and allowed themselves to be roughly searched for weapons, and then marched toward the town, surrounded by the group of Frenchmen.

"Are you at war with these other people?" Carl asked Jules, a lanky man almost as tall as Chester, who was walking beside him.

"They are at war with us," Jules said. "They are at war with everybody. You do not know about the Boche?"

"We don't have them in our sector," Carl said.

"What a wonderful place that must be," Jules replied.

"Why don't you wear uniforms?" Carl asked. "I thought you had to wear uniforms; it was like one of the rules."

"The Boche have taught us that there are no rules," Jules said. "We are the Maquis, and we fight the Boche. Whatever we wear, wherever we go, whatever we do, we fight the Boche. That is our life."

The people in the town, when they entered it, were calmly going about their business of putting out the fires and taking care of the wounded. The dead were lined up in the main street, under blankets.

The young tank driver was turned over to the mayor of the town, and Carl, Chester, and O'Malley were taken to a stone cellar in a bombed warehouse to be interrogated.

The questioning went around and around for a while. The French attitude was that it was a trick, and they just wanted to find out what sort of trick it was before they took them out and shot them. It was not an attitude that allowed Carl to feel at all relaxed in his confinement.

Chester finally came up with the only thing he could think of that would establish their story: he offered to show the Maquis leader the trick of going through the barrier.

"I should have done that anyway," he told Carl. "It's the best possible way to undermine the whole system. I should have started giving lessons months ago."

"You teach two men how to penetrate the barrier," Pierre decided, "and we'll send them out tonight to try. If they don't come back, or if only one comes back and he says the other died at the barrier, then we shoot you tomorrow morning. Is this agreeable?"

"What if they do come back?" Chester asked.

"Then we talk further," Pierre said.

"Bring on your men," Chester said, shrugging.

"I go ask for volunteers," Pierre told him.

They were given the freedom of the cellar, such as it was, for the night while the two young men who had volunteered went off to test Chester's method. They had been dubious, but willing. *Dulce et decorum est pro patria mori*.

Carl was sound asleep on the thin blanket that separated him from the stone floor when the sounds of gunfire and shouting from above woke him. First the gunfire, then the shouting. About a minute later, which gave him just enough time to get his shoes back on, a group of men broke through the cellar door and raced down, waving lanterns and sweeping the dingy room with their beams. One of them prodded O'Malley, who was still sleeping, sharply with his boot, and they herded them upstairs. About five of the Maquis members had also been captured, and were grouped together with their hands up, staring sullenly into the lights.

Their captors had black uniforms with silver piping, silver stripes, and shiny silver insignia. They looked very efficient.

The group of them, Maquis and Confederates, were herded out into the street, where a large truck waited. The Maquis members were forced to climb up onto the back of the truck. Just as Chester was about to join them, a voice from the dark interrupted:

"Just a second," it said, "I want those three." A black-clad Inspector walked into the light. "I've been looking for you for some time," he told Chester.

❋ 15 ❋

They were handcuffed together and loaded aboard a large flitterboat by three Inspectors holding slender silver rods that somehow looked more menacing than any of the hand weapons Carl had seen in the past weeks.

"You've given us quite a run," the chief Inspector said. "But we've got you now. The question is, what are we to do with you?"

"How'd you find us?" Chester asked.

"Oh, you left a back trail that was easy enough to follow, if you have the proper instruments," the chief Inspector said. "The only thing is, it's quite time-consuming. We almost lost you when you went through the barrier. The boys didn't know you could do that, so they spent quite a bit of time snuffling around on the near side trying to pick up your trail. Should have guessed, though, you've done it before. We always assumed you hopped over, or stole a flitter. After all, you did once steal a flitter."

"Hopped over?" Carl asked.

The chief Inspector turned to stare at him. "Yes, that's what we call it. The only thing is, it takes a couple of days, usually, to prepare for it. If you don't know how to do it, I'd best not tell you."

"What are ye going to do with us?" O'Malley asked.

"Yes, that is the problem. We didn't think anyone could escape from Devil's Island, after all. The Governor General wants to see the three of you. But after he's through with you ... Well, we'll have to think of something, won't we?" He smiled and went back up to the control compartment.

"Wait a minute," Chester called.

The chief Inspector came back to the doorway. "What?" he asked.

"The Governor General wants to see us?"

"That's right."

"The Governor General of what?" Carl asked.

"Of Earth," the chief Inspector said. "His château is right near here. We'll be there in a few minutes."

"Earth?" Chester said.

"That's right."

"Then you don't know either."

"What's that?"

"Do you know why the Governor General wants to see me?" Chester asked.

"No," the chief Inspector said.

"Because I know a secret that frightens him," Chester said. "He doesn't want anyone on this planet to know it, and I do."

"That's interesting," the chief Inspector said, unconvinced.

"Do you want to know what it is?" Chester asked, smiling up at him.

"No, I guess not," the chief Inspector said, and hastily backed out and slammed the door between the compartments.

Chester began to laugh. In a minute he was rolling around on the floor, holding his sides, unable to stop. O'Malley, who was handcuffed to him, was getting pulled around, so he sat on his large friend until he calmed down.

They landed on the lawn of the estate, with the great manor house in the background. It was all lighted up, and through the large French doors they could see people dancing. It was a costume party with all the ages of Earth represented. There were pharaohs and Eskimos, Roman senators and Southern governors, veiled dancing girls and tutued ballerinas.

And, Carl saw as he was led past the windows, there was Alyssaunde. Dressed like a peasant girl in silk and satin, dancing with a lordling in a high stiff collar, there was Alyssaunde! And she saw him. She turned away as she was spun around by her partner, but she turned back while he was still in sight. And she winked. Slowly, and clearly, she winked her right eye.

Then they were past the windows.

They were taken to a side door that led directly down a flight of stone stairs to a cellar with a row of stone, barred holding cells. They were thrust into one of the cells, still handcuffed together, and the door was slammed and bolted. "We'll tell the Governor General you're here," the chief Inspector said. "Good night, and thank you for a most pleasant chase." He raised his hat to them, and he and his men left the cellar.

"I don't think I like this cellar as much as the last cellar," O'Malley said.

"I don't like the idea that I'm becoming a connoisseur of cellars," Chester said.

"Alyssaunde's here," Carl said; "she's upstairs. I saw her."

"How nice for you," Chester said.

"She winked at me," Carl said.

Chester shook his head. "She had a dust mote in her eye," he said. "Or worse, she did wink at you. Think nothing of it. Don't let it bother you."

"Get some sleep, lad," O'Malley said, "Ye're going to need it."

"She'll help," Carl said.

Chester looked at him strangely. "Don't you know who she is?" he asked. "I remembered while we were in her boat, but there was no point in bringing it up."

"What do you mean?" Carl said.

"Her name is Flortnoy-Bobsmite. Alyssaunde Flortnoy-Bobsmite."

"So?" Carl asked.

"Her father, Sir Andrew Flortnoy-Bobsmite, is the Governor General of Earth. The gentleman who wants to see us."

"Oh," Carl said.

Alyssaunde appeared in the doorway. "Here," she said, thrusting a bundle of clothing through the bars, "put these on. I'll have to take you upstairs through the party to get you out of here."

"What are ye doing here?" O'Malley asked. "What sort of trick is this?"

"No trick," Alyssaunde said. "I heard my father talking to some of his advisers. He plans to interrogate you and then either thrust you away in a dungeon below Government House, or have you killed." She turned to Chester. "And I found out that what you told me was true. They locked you up just because you know something. And I found out what it was.

"I tried to get in touch with you on Devil's Island, but I'm not very good at that sort of thing. The Inspectors turned my flitterboat away."

"That was you, then?" Carl said.

"Yes," she said. "Are you all right? All of you?"

"Can you really get us out of here?" Chester asked.

"With a little luck," she said. "Who can tell who's wearing these costumes? I'll get you up to my flitter on the roof, and we'll leave."

"Won't you get in trouble?"

"I don't plan to come back either," Alyssaunde said. "Everyone's been lying to me all my life, and I'd like to find out the truth."

"You've convinced me," Chester said, grabbing the bundle on the floor. "What about these handcuffs?"

"Oh," Alyssaunde said. "I didn't know. You're all

handcuffed together. There's no way to sneak through this building with you all handcuffed together. Not in the middle of the Anniversary Party."

"The anniversary of what?" Chester asked.

"I don't know, they've never told me," Alyssaunde said. "Wait here, I'll see if I can get a key. Get those costumes on." And she disappeared from the door.

"Wait here, she says," O'Malley grumbled. "Very funny."

"Where's she going to get a key from?" Carl wondered, unwrapping his costume.

Chester shrugged. "Maybe she used to play with handcuffs as a little girl," he suggested. "Maybe she does escape tricks. Maybe she has a boyfriend who's an Inspector."

"Oh," Carl said.

The costumes were not merely sets of clothes from various sectors, they were identified with different historical characters. At least Carl assumed they were historical characters, although neither he nor his friends had ever heard of them. The names of the characters were sewn into the neckbands of the costumes. Carl's was a suit something like the one O'Malley had been wearing, but somehow more angular, and the name sewn into it was John Dillinger.

Different O'Malley fit into his clothes as if he had been born to wear them. They were very much like what he wore at home, he said, but better made. The name sewn into them was Robin Hood.

Chester A. Arthur had more of a problem. The costume was complex, and it was not readily apparent how some of the items were to be worn. But when he was finished, with the skintight pants, the boots, the cape, and the magnificent plumed hat, he looked like a heroic, larger-than-life figure, subject of some great epic. Of course his six-and-a-half-foot height helped. The name sewn into the back of his cape was Cyrano de Bergerac.

Alyssaunde returned to the doorway. "A slight problem," she said.

"You couldn't get the key," Chester said.

Alyssaunde looked at him. "You should always dress like that," she told him. "No, that's not it. Here's the key." She passed it through the bars. "There's a guard at the head of the stairs. I could get down, being who I am, but I can't bring you back up if I didn't go down with you. And I think he's suspicious. But he can't do anything about that till he's relieved—he has to stay at that door."

Chester unlocked the handcuffs and passed the key to O'Malley. "You're doing fine," he told Alyssaunde. "Let us take care of the guard."

Alyssaunde pulled the bolt for the door, and it swung open. "It's up to you," she said.

"Let me," O'Malley said.

Chester gave him a courtly bow. "My guest," he said.

O'Malley staggered to the staircase and started up. "I'm having a bit o' the whisky," he wailed. "Ye're having a touch o' the a rye,/We'll have us a smack o' the brandy,/Then lay us both down and die!"

"What's that?" the guard shouted from above. "What's going on down there?"

"Aye, old friend," O'Malley called. "Turn that light down a bit, will ye? It hurts my eyes."

"What light?" the guard asked, trying to figure out where this drunk had come from. O'Malley had almost reached him now.

"It doesn't matter," O'Malley said. "I'm chugging a flask o' the aquavit,/Yer glugging the absinthe straight down. . . ." He had reached the guard, and one massive arm shot out and grasped the guard's throat, and the guard was down.

"Quick now," Alyssaunde said. "Up to the roof. This way!"

❊ 16 ❊

Carl had never seen anything like Sanloo, nor imagined that anything like it existed. Sanloo was the outpost city of an interstellar civilization. Everything about it was chaotic, jumbled, and huge. Tall, slender pryoconcrete spires leaped up away from squat, hulking steel and stone fortresses. Great transparent domes with fairyland gardens of alien plants crowded against rows of squalid brownstone tenements. Narrow twisting streets led into broad boulevards. And everywhere a network of canals divided the city into island fragments, which developed individual characters of their own.

And outside the city, clearly visible from the high rooftop landing area on which Alyssaunde had set the flitter down, was the spaceport: acre after acre of flat gray pyroconcrete speckled with flat round buildings painted violent red, and dotted with symmetrical rows of landing pits. And in the pits, over half a hundred spacecraft of all the patterns and varieties then in use in the known galaxy: sleek private speedsters with stubby, knife-edge wings; bulbous freighters with their concentric circles of rocket nozzles sticking out from under the landing cowl; strange alien craft whose colors and angles were peculiar to human eyes.

"What do you think?" Alyssaunde asked.

Carl pulled his gaze away from the spaceport. "I would never have believed," he said. "I never would have thought it possible...."

TOMORROW KNIGHT 155

"And we are a backward planet," Chester said. "With a small tourist trade, and little commerce. Can you imagine what civilization must be like?"

"We have to take ground transportation into the spaceport," Alyssaunde said. "They don't allow flitterboats to fly over, for obvious reasons."

"It seems so strange," Carl said. "I mean, I knew intellectually that we weren't all there was to the universe, and the Guests came from somewhere else. But to stand here staring at the ships that actually fly between these worlds. I mean, somehow I feel very small."

"I know just what you mean," Chester told him. "I, also, have a queasy and insignificant feeling at the sight of the ships that sail the stars."

Alyssaunde put her hands on Carl's face, cupping his cheeks. "Is it so terrible, Carl, learning that there's so much more to the universe than you had thought?"

"Terrible?" Carl echoed. He sensed that Alyssaunde's face was close to his own, felt the softness of her hands. "No, not terrible. It's—I think it's the most wonderful thing that's ever happened to me, learning that there's so much—so much—so much *everything*. It's even greater than being made a knight-brevet by the king. But it's kind of scary. I mean—all at once, you know."

"Aye, 'tis a great thing to learn that the world isn't just yer little sector," Different O'Malley interjected, "and a greater thing to learn that the universe isn't just yer own little world. But what are we goin' to *do* about it, friends?"

Alyssaunde dropped her hands from Carl's cheeks and whirled to face O'Malley. "We're going to steal a spaceship. That's what we're going to do about it. And we're going to escape from this phony Earth, the four of us, and make our way to the *real* Earth!"

"That sounds mighty good to me," O'Malley responded. "Don't stop now, though. Once we get to the real Earth, what do you propose that we do? Go into hiding? Start a revolution? Take over the government?"

"Let's take that as we come to it," Chester said. "The important thing now is to get started."

"What ship do we take?" Carl asked. "Does any of us know how to manage a ship?"

"My father's," Alyssaunde said. "And I'm a rated pilot in it. It's right over there." She pointed to a tall, slender craft near the entrance to the spaceport.

Chester nodded. "Let's go," he said.

Nobody even gave them a second look as they went through the streets. The guard at the gate to the spaceport saluted Alyssaunde as they went by.

"This is so easy," Chester said. "I'm afraid I must be dreaming."

They climbed up the ladder to the ship, and O'Maley paused to look around. "It's somehow hard to say good-bye, regardless," he said.

"Don't say good-bye," Chester said. "We'll be back."

DAW BOOKS

- [ ] **THE WHENABOUTS OF BURR by Michael Kurland.** DAW celebrates the Bicentennial with an account of Emperor Burr and President Alexander Hamilton!
(#UY1182—$1.25)

- [ ] **ONE-EYE by Stuart Gordon.** In the name of the Mutant Godling, it is flight—or fight! A complex and brilliant vision of a far future. (#UQ1077—95¢)

- [ ] **TWO-EYES by Stuart Gordon.** The vibrations of mutation were shaking a world and bringing to birth a new one.
(#UY1135—$1.25)

- [ ] **THREE-EYES by Stuart Gordon.** The final culmination!
(#UW1206—$1.50)

- [ ] **THE BIRTHGRAVE by Tanith Lee.** "A big, rich, bloody swords-and-sorcery epic with a truly memorable heroine —as tough as Conan the Barbarian but more convincing."—*Publishers Weekly.* (#UW1177—$1.50)

- [ ] **TIME SLAVE by John Norman.** The creator of Gor recreates the days of the caveman in a vivid new novel of time travel and human destiny. (#UW1204—$1.50)

DAW BOOKS are represented by the publishers of Signet and Mentor Books, THE NEW AMERICAN LIBRARY, INC.

THE NEW AMERICAN LIBRARY, INC.,
P.O. Box 999, Bergenfield, New Jersey 07621

Please send me the DAW BOOKS I have checked above. I am enclosing
$_____(check or money order—no currency or C.O.D.'s).
Please include the list price plus 25¢ a copy to cover mailing costs.

Name_____

Address_____

City_____State_____Zip Code_____

Please allow at least 3 weeks for delivery

DAW sf BOOKS

☐ **THE R-MASTER by Gordon R. Dickson.** Russian roulette for the mind—winner takes the world!
(#UY1155—$1.25)

☐ **SLEEPWALKER'S WORLD by Gordon R. Dickson.** "An astronaut returns to Earth to find it immobilized by a mysterious power. The year's best . . ."—Philadelphia Inquirer.
(#UY1192—$1.25)

☐ **THE STAR ROAD by Gordon R. Dickson.** An unforgettable collection of Dickson's best space tales.
(#UY1127—$1.25)

☐ **DORSAI! by Gordon R. Dickson.** The really Big novel of the mercenary soldiers in its first unabridged paperback edition.
(#UW1218—$1.50)

☐ **TACTICS OF MISTAKE by Gordon R. Dickson.** The first of the great DORSAI novels is a major sf classic.
(#UQ1009—95¢)

☐ **SOLDIER, ASK NOT by Gordon Dickson.** One of his great DORSAI novels back in print by public demand.
(#UW1207—$1.50)

DAW BOOKS are represented by the publishers of Signet and Mentor Books, THE NEW AMERICAN LIBRARY, INC.

THE NEW AMERICAN LIBRARY, INC.,
P.O. Box 999, Bergenfield, New Jersey 07621

Please send me the DAW BOOKS I have checked above. I am enclosing
$_____ (check or money order—no currency or C.O.D.'s).
Please include the list price plus 25¢ a copy to cover mailing costs.

Name_____

Address_____

City_____ State_____ Zip Code_____
Please allow at least 3 weeks for delivery

DAW BOOKS sf

DAW PRESENTS MICHAEL CONEY

Theodore Sturgeon wrote of Coney that "it is heartening to see a good writer become very good."

- ☐ **RAX.** The coming of the cold sun meant the ending of their world ... or such it seemed. A truly different novel!
(#UY1205—$1.25)

- ☐ **THE JAWS THAT BITE, THE CLAWS THAT CATCH.** A symphony of sharks, bondswomen, and a social crisis in times to come. (#UY1163—$1.25)

- ☐ **THE HERO OF DOWNWAYS.** Though they cloned for courage, it took more than breeding to find the light.
(#UQ1070—95¢)

- ☐ **MONITOR FOUND IN ORBIT.** An outstanding collection of the best stories of this rising light of science fiction.
(#UQ1132—95¢)

- ☐ **FRIENDS COME IN BOXES.** The epic story of one deathless day in 2256 A.D. (#UQ1056—95¢)

- ☐ **MIRROR IMAGE.** They could be either your most beloved object or your living nightmare! (#UQ1031—95¢)

DAW BOOKS are represented by the publishers of Signet and Mentor Books, THE NEW AMERICAN LIBRARY, INC.

THE NEW AMERICAN LIBRARY, INC.,
P.O. Box 999, Bergenfield, New Jersey 07621

Please send me the DAW BOOKS I have checked above. I am enclosing
$_____(check or money order—no currency or C.O.D.'s).
Please include the list price plus 25¢ a copy to cover mailing costs.

Name_____

Address_____

City_____State_____Zip Code_____
Please allow at least 3 weeks for delivery

DAW BOOKS

Presenting the saga of Earl Dumarest's search for Terra—the greatest work of a great science fiction writer:

☐ **MAYENNE by E. C. Tubb.** An eternal riddle is posed by the planet that masquerades as human!
(#UQ1054—95¢)

☐ **JONDELLE by E. C. Tubb.** Dumarest's trail to Lost Terra leads through a city of paranoid kidnappers.
(#UQ1075—95¢)

☐ **ZENYA by E. C. Tubb.** Dumarest commands her army as the price of a bit of Earth fable. (#UQ1126—95¢)

☐ **ELOISE by E. C. Tubb.** The twelfth of the Dumarest novels brings that rugged traveler closer to his goal.
(#UY1162—$1.25)

☐ **EYE OF THE ZODIAC by E. C. Tubb.** At last Dumarest finds a world that knows the Terrestrial zodiac!
(#UY1194—$1.25)

DAW BOOKS are represented by the publishers of Signet and Mentor Books, THE NEW AMERICAN LIBRARY, INC.

THE NEW AMERICAN LIBRARY, INC.,
P.O. Box 999, Bergenfield, New Jersey 07621

Please send me the DAW BOOKS I have checked above. I am enclosing
$_____(check or money order—no currency or C.O.D.'s).
Please include the list price plus 25¢ a copy to cover mailing costs.

Name_____

Address_____

City_____State_____Zip Code_____
Please allow at least 3 weeks for delivery